AF279285

KRISTEN GLEASON

THE WALLET

AND OTHER THEFTS

Fonograf Editions
Edited by Ellena Basada, Jeff Alessandrelli & Adie B. Steckel
Portland, OR & New York City, NY

First Edition, First Printing
FONO43

Published by Fonograf Editions
www.fonografeditions.com

For information about permission to reuse any material from this book,
please contact Fonograf Ed. at info@fonografeditions.com.

Distributed by NYU Press
NYUPress.org

The manufacturer's authorized representative in the EU for product
safety is Mare Nostrum Group B.V., Mauritskade 21D, 1091 GC
Amsterdam, The Netherlands.
Email: gpsr@mare-nostrum.co.uk.

[clmp]

Fonograf Editions is a proud member of the Community
of Literary Magazines and Presses

ISBN: 978-1-964499-67-3
ISBN (ebook): 978-1-964499-68-0
LCCN: 2025943567

THE WALLET
& OTHER THEFTS

FONOGRAF EDITIONS

CONTENTS

I was right not to fear any thief but myself,
who will end by leaving me with nothing.

—KATHERINE ANNE PORTER

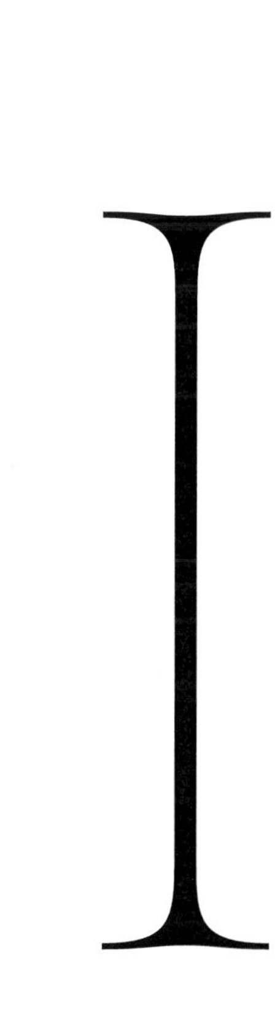

The Café

THREE WOMEN SAT TOGETHER AT AN OUTDOOR café. The walls of their semi-private cell were made of curtains, sheer ones—in turquoise, pink, and gold. There was no ceiling. The sun was out. It was really very pleasant weather, but because it was one of those cafés that just make you want to transcend, dissolve, advance, et cetera, there were no other customers present, so the women could be, in their comportment, as they really were: quite free.

They sank into low cushions around a bright white slab of table, their knees buckling up close to their chins, and ordered confidently from the waiter, who was always away but never sufficiently gone, decaffeinated coffee with cream.

The cream came to the table in a handmade ceramic, the bottom rounded so it wouldn't sit flat. A spill seemed imminent, and the café didn't help, being spirit-like, always responding to its wavy medium, so the cream sloshed out of the ceramic, and the women couldn't stop it, not even with their minds.

The waiter reappeared at once. He was not handsome, but he was exceedingly unpleasant, so their instinct was to treat him very well, by groveling.

"I'm so clumsy this morning," said Ava, as the waiter folded neatly at the waist and wiped the cream from the table. "I shouldn't be allowed to live."

He nodded and vanished through a shifting wall of curtain.

The women did not seem to watch him go, but they knew everything about how he went. Posturally, they had an ease, as if they had slept together, woken up together, walked to the café together, and would someday merge together, when it came time for that, into the triple-sided god they felt sure they would someday become.

"I'm getting that itch," said Ava. "I'm feeling exactly like a prisoner. I need to take a trip."

"But you're already on a trip!" said Eve, winking. "Where are you going to go?"

"Romania, I imagine."

"Do you know anyone in Romania?" asked Ovelle.

"No. That would ruin it, don't you think?"

The women nodded.

"Even thinking about it," said Ava, "I start to feel free. Even just anticipating, in extreme detail, the Romanian landscape I haven't seen, even drawing it with my own thoughts, inside of my own brain, where there is no eraser, makes me feel like I've already been there. But I'll still go, to make sure I'm right."

"I should take a trip too," said Ovelle. "Otherwise how could I claim to have lived these past three months?"

"You couldn't," said Eve.

"I couldn't!" said Ovelle.

"Where are *you* thinking of going?" asked Ava.

"God, I don't know. Somewhere no one would ever guess I would want to go. Somewhere that would really destroy my personality," said Ovelle, "and then remake it in someone else's image."

"But whose?" asked Ava.

The waiter returned. He delivered a plate of seedy crackers, then flowed out through an opposite slit. The women laughed.

"The service here is unreal!"

A warm breeze lifted the walls of curtain—turquoise, pink, gold—and dragged the sheerness over the faces of the women. The combination was rite-like. They were the color of a multi-nodal sex organ, gilded.

"We are the buried tool of someone else's afterlife," exclaimed Ava. "And we have been unearthed!"

But they were not dead, or even dying. On the contrary—they seemed to have too much of life.

"Maybe South Korea," said Ovelle, arranging the curtains back into walls.

"I've always wanted to go there," said Eve. "Maybe I'll go after you go."

"I'll leave no trace," said Ovelle. "I promise. The country will be untouched, by me. Only *I* will be changed."

The three nodded gravely.

"Do you remember my Egypt story?" said Ava.

"There were so many stories from your Egypt trip. Remind me," said Eve.

"There *were* so many stories. That trip was pure meaning. But I'm talking about the dream I had in Egypt. The story of that dream."

"Sounds familiar, but tell it again. Why else are we in a café?"

"Exactly. I was in Egypt. I'd spent all evening with youth organizers, revolutionaries, when it happened. They'd been trying to build up to something, something momentous and consequential, but then the build-up culminated prematurely in a single event: a dramatic reading. This reading, of a secret list, happened late that night, in someone's underground home. The list was of 198 methods of nonviolence. Each item in the list was chanted, emotionally, by a person so tall he looked sick. I laughed the whole way through, but the youths didn't seem to mind. They seemed to understand how I might feel, as someone who was not from there, about this kind of recitation. But I was being a real shithead, which I forgive myself for, because it was a lesson about me that I couldn't have learned in any other way than by taking that trip and laughing at those kids, but I don't have to tell that to any of you.

"In the end it was worth it, but that doesn't erase my bad behavior. I do know that. I'm not a total monster—I *can* reflect. Anyway, back at the hotel after the reading, I stood on the balcony in a long violet nightgown. I had no idea who had sent the gown. It was sitting outside of my room when I got there, on the floor in a shallow box, so I just slipped it on. That's the way things were back then. Unknown senders—they positively proliferated. I think I assumed it was a suitor who would otherwise never materialize, and you know how I am, that was fine with me. Out there, on the balcony late at night, with no underwear on, I felt mentally large. I could remember many items from the list, but they didn't seem so funny anymore. The items had organized, somehow, against me. But this was wrong, I was their friend! It was all supposed to be very funny!

"*Delivering symbolic objects. Wearing of symbols. Symbolic lights. Symbolic sounds. Symbolic reclamations.* Why could I not stop remembering the list, and why was I taking it so personally? Was it the gown? Had I unwittingly put on the vestment of revolution? And if so, why, now, did I never want to take it off? I started to panic. Would someone try to take the gown from me? Would they come, even there, to my room, which I had paid for, to get it back? I had never wanted anything so badly as I wanted to keep that gown. It was my *clothing* (I finally understood the word). It had become, in the space of an hour, the only possible outfit for me!

"I got into bed, pulled the covers up tight. The list pursued me. *Total personal noncooperation. Stay-at-home. Lysistratic nonaction.* It started to become very clear: The youths had got it all wrong. They would never succeed by reciting that list. They had to *interpret* it, which in that particular case, meant doing the opposite of what it said. It was blasphemy what they had done, speaking the items out loud, without qualification, as if they were facts—the last facts! It was contra-revolutionary!

"Lying there, I determined that I was going to help them with their revolution. I would set them on the right course, I fully intended to—I was in a state—and I was about to jump out of bed and go back to that underground home to tell them exactly what they needed to do, but then my mind began to drift. I started to think of my young lover, the one who left me for someone exactly my age. Remember him? Had I been fair to him, I wondered, when I sent him that little note? I had known it would stick in him forever, like a barb, just infecting him with doubt when all I'd really wanted was to dismantle him for a single brilliant second with some custom-made attention (I always intended for him to recover).

"No, it had not been fair, that note. He'd been so right to leave me—I had no intention of taking care of my body or my skin. I *wanted* to look old and he was incredibly superficial. It wouldn't have worked out. So why did I send the note? And why did I also, into the envelope that contained the note, slip a small green gem that had been in my vagina? And why did I then deliver the note, by hand, to his parents' house, knowing how he felt about his parents? Poor thing—I had ruined him! With all this on my mind, I have no idea how I fell asleep, but I did, eventually, still wearing the gown. And that's when I had the dream.

"I was lying in the bottom of a cup. My throbbing groin subtended a thistle. It was, or I was, flowering. As a being, my function was to embrace, to enclose, but also to bloom. It was all very obvious, I thought so even then, as my dreaming self. It was all simply gorged with meaning. But I was happy, in the dream. I knew my function, and I performed it well.

"Two men, in dull crowns, peered into the cup. I was picked up, or the cup was, by these men. They passed the cup back and forth.

Good work, Ava, said one of them. *You do such good work.*

Don't praise her, said the other. *It'll ruin the bloom.*

There's no such thing as a too-proud bloom. There's only such thing as a humble bloom, which stinks.

"The men began to fight over the cup I was in. I was tossed all around, and my groin was grasping at the thistle, but it wasn't strong enough. The thistle slipped out, and from the gaping hole in me came a blinding light, a real cock-slam of a big golden ray. It was a vision! Knocked their crowns right off. Bored partway into their skulls so that their heads were living grottos, not empty. Not at all. There was snow in there. Lots of it. And little people on skis. But I did not want to go in there. I just didn't.

"When I woke up, it was clear to me that I had to leave Egypt at once. The gown was gone, and I was naked. Someone's gnarled stick, not mine, leaned next to the door. I went to the bathroom, and when I came back the stick was gone. The next day, I traveled to Switzerland, where I saw a dog drown in the most beautiful lake I had ever seen. And that is still the case. I've yet to see a lake that can beat that one in Switzerland for beauty."

"I think I do remember that story," said Ovelle. "But hearing it again, I feel I've learned something new. What a fount travel is."

"What a boon."

"I pity anyone who's never left home," said Eve. "And to be honest, I judge them too."

"But wasn't there more?" said Ovelle. "To that story? Something else happened in Egypt, didn't it? I seem to remember there was some other thing."

"In Egypt? Not that I can recall. I left that morning, so it was just an airport day for me."

The waiter materialized in their cell. "More decaf?" he asked.

He looked straight ahead, his chin rough as a rock, his mouth singularly unenticing. He blinked, and the café flickered on and off. He touched, discreetly, the secret defect of his outfit—the exposed and tooth-torn zipper of his fly.

"Why, yes," said Ava. "I'll have another."

"And me," said Eve.

"And one for me, too," said Ovelle.

"Do you feel," said Ava, when he was gone, "like I feel? Like he doesn't want us here, but only so he can *act* like he doesn't want us here? I almost apologized just now—just for having come!"

"Never apologize for visiting a place," said Eve. "I can't stand to hear anyone debase experience."

"Yes, experience is neutral," said Ava, "or it is virtuous. Those are the only things that experience can be."

Ovelle cleared her throat. "You are so right. Like one time I went to Caucasia in the dead of winter. The hotel was empty except for one other woman with an infant. She walked the halls all night wailing with grief, the child screaming too. We met only once, in the drab hallway, when I was on my way to the shared bathroom. She pleaded with me in a language I didn't understand. She kept pointing at my left eye, which had begun to water uncontrollably at the idea that this woman might actually touch it. Normally, this kind of accidental antagonism would have been completely inexcusable to me, but in this particular situation, I found it very easy to endure. I tried to take the baby from her, and she let me. She stopped crying and sat on the floor. I sat next to her, singing to the baby, cooing at it, tickling its toes. Then she started to use her hands to communicate. She moved them in front of us in the hallway, painting a picture in the air that I could read. She was crying, her hands said, because she'd written a book that described a coming catastrophe. It wasn't fiction, she insisted. It was very real but it read just like a novel. She had lost this prophetic text during the course of her travels. It had been stolen by a man who had also stolen her scarf—she showed me her neck, red from exposure. This man, whom she'd met at a very different sort of café than the one we're sitting in now, had revealed to her a few details about his itinerary, which was why she was in this particular hotel—she was following him. She hoped to find him and get her book back. She didn't care about seeing Caucasia, or about recovering her scarf, even though her grandmother had given it to her. She cared only about the book, which would be misunderstood if she couldn't accompany it wherever it went, if she couldn't, as the author, provide the genre: nonfiction, prophetic. The book was the truth, she said, but the man was probably reading it right now as if it were a novel. If she couldn't find it and impress upon anyone who read it that it was not just something she'd made up, thousands of people would die."

"Did she ever find him?" asked Eve.

"That's the thing: I don't know."

"See? Neutral," said Ava.

"Yeah, like once I met a beggar on the streets of Valparaiso," said Eve. "He was deeply concerned for a tree that was growing, or really failing to grow, in the center of a courtyard there. It was old, he said, nobody knew how old it was, it had always been there—so why was it dying now? Why did he, the beggar, have the bad luck of being alive to witness the death of this tree that had seemed, for generations of people, to be eternal? I took him to a café not at all like this one and bought him some bread, which he didn't touch. I asked him if he'd like to shower back in my hotel room, and he said yes. While he showered, I tried to lure a bird through the window with the bread I bought, and when he emerged from the shower and saw what I was doing he smacked the bread out of my hand. I fell onto the bed, but he wasn't interested in sex. His skin was a totally different color than it had been before the shower. *What is love if it isn't this?* I said, and he started to cry. *You remind me of my most recent boss*, he said. *She was very cruel to me, to the last. She died beneath me in bed.*

"We spent the night together, not fucking. We told each other everything, all about our childhoods and our dreams. In the morning, I went out and bought him some rope, then left him alone for a few hours. I fully expected that he would hang himself, but when I got back to the room he was still there, sitting on the bed, surrounded by a small crowd of people, who were draped all over each other on the floor. He was giving a lecture on the reductions of Paraguay. The reductions were some sort of strategy-cum-building, where people were instructed in methods of dehumanizing nature I think. Maybe I can't remember exactly, or I didn't understand some of the Spanish because I wasn't really listening. He was whipping the rope around as he spoke, and it was mesmerizing because the rope was not behaving like an object at all, but like something aspirational, something with muscle and heart. The tail end curled around his neck, caressed it, let it go. The rope was showing what it *could* do—kill him—but would not, because it loved this beggar, who was its master. The crowd kept reaching for the beggar's feet. Coyly, he kept moving them out of reach, then extending them again, then removing them, and so on. He never allowed them to make contact, but neither did he convince them that they should stop trying. My boat was leaving in an hour, so I handed him the key to the room. He took it without looking at me and said, *It's the least you could do.* On my way to the port, I told the driver to take me to the tree, the one that was dying, in a courtyard somewhere. *It was supposed to be eternal? I said. An eternal tree? But now it's dying?* The driver shook his head. *Your guidebook must be old. That tree died years ago. Someone hung himself from it, and then his mother came out in the middle of the night and cut it down. All by herself. With an axe!*"

"Virtuous," said Ava.

A cell phone rang, and she took it from her purse, crossed her legs, held it a few inches from her ear. "I'm having a lovely time, yes, I'm at this wild café, it seems to be made entirely of air. There's really nothing urgent, is there? Nothing pressing? I mean, I'm on vacation. Yes. Right. This is travel. Thank you for saying that. Nice to talk to you too."

She hung up the phone and turned excitedly to the other women. "So as I was saying: Should we take a trip?"

"We are overdue. But it really depends, I should think, on the forecast," said Ovelle.

The waiter arrived with their refills.

The lean of his delivery was unnecessarily extreme. His fingers lingered on the last saucer, pinching it suggestively. "Travel is a boat," he said, tucking his tray beneath his arm, "that floats on the sea of heaven and never sinks." Then he slipped through the curtains again.

Eve huffed. "A riddle. How rude."

"Check please!" shouted Ava.

This time, the waiter did not come right away. The women, in anticipation, inched forward on their low cushions. With their knees, they steadied themselves against the low white table. At last, the waiter arrived. His eyes closed and his thin nose held aloft, he presented an abalone shell containing the bill.

"Whenever you're ready," he said. "However, the café is closed and has been for some time. You can see that there's nobody else here. But please don't hurry—there's no rush."

"Here you go," said Ava, tossing a single coin into the shell. The coin was a shifting color. Pink played over its surface, then gold, then turquoise. Neither side was marked. The edges of the coin were smooth and tapered toward an impossible thinness.

The waiter carefully examined the coin. "I'm sorry, ladies," he said. "But we can't accept this."

The women jumped. Eve locked the waiter in a strange embrace, twisting his body, so that Ovelle, with a kick to the back of his knees, was able to send him all the way down to the table, which was so far down, being so very low, that when he hit the surface, the result was spectacular. What had appeared so permanent—that broad white surface, flawless as a field of salt—turned out to be anything but. The table splintered, its particulate interior was revealed, and the waiter lay supine in the midst of the debris. His eyes were shocked, even hurt, and he grimaced in pain.

Ava jumped onto his chest, Ovelle had his arm, Eve was on his feet. He stopped struggling and stared plaintively up at the sky.

"All currency is accepted everywhere," said Ava. "You know that."

"We *will* travel," said Ovelle. "We *will* go here and there. You can't stop us."

The waiter was moving his lips around, perhaps working up the courage to speak.

"We're not tourists," said Ava. She signaled to Ovelle. "It doesn't have to be vicious or dramatic," she said. "Just the right amount of pressure should do it. Fact is, that coin is very sharp." She drew a line across the waiter's throat with her finger.

"Wait," he said finally. "Can I tell you something?"

"That depends," said Ava.

"It's about a trip I once took," he said.

The women were curious. They agreed to listen, but they would not relinquish their superior position.

"Okay," said Ava. "Go for it."

"I once took a trip to Japan. I'd wanted to go for years and had worked and worked to afford it. On the flight over, I got very sick. When I arrived, it was all I could do to get off the plane. I spent four nights on the floor of the arrivals terminal, unable to summon the energy to ask for help. A young boy visited me during my illness. He wore the feet of a goose and the hands of a beautiful woman. He applied a cooling balm to my cracked lips, balanced a hollow apple on my stomach, then disappeared. When I finally had the strength, I opened the apple, which was neatly hinged, and saw that the inside was an exact replica of my childhood home. My father was lying prone at the bottom of the stairs, not moving, and my mother was watching TV in the living room. I wasn't there, but I wanted to be. So I tried very hard and soon I was. In my room. How I had missed it! I looked around at all my objects—the seed crystal, the thunder egg, the giant quartz. Then I walked the hallway slowly. It was dark. I ran my hand along the wall until I felt the banister. I stopped at the top of the stairs. I could see the outline of my father's body at the bottom. I called down to him: *What are you doing? Did you fall again?* He didn't respond. Instead my mother's voice floated in from the living room. *He's reflecting on his life,* she said, *and on what he's done to deserve it.* And then, just like that, I was back in the airport, the apple rushing toward me. I bit it hard, to defend myself against the impact. It was instinct. I don't like apples. But once I'd started biting, I couldn't stop. I ate the entire thing, even the core, even my childhood home, even my parents. When I had finished, I realized: I had forgotten to eat me. It was on the flight back home that it hit me, what that trip to Japan had meant. It meant that I might never die. I might never die. I might never die. I might never…"

Ovelle slapped her hand over the waiter's mouth. "There's no point in killing him," she said. "He's already finished." She flipped the coin into the air and did not catch it. "Now I remember what it was about Egypt."

"Yeah?" said Ava. "Tell me."

"You said you got very ill there, with some sort of fever only foreigners get."

"Oh," said Ava. "That's right. But then I thought of travel and came back to life."

The women relaxed into the cushions. The waiter rolled onto his side and spun the coin among the loose shards of what had previously been a table. "But it is *like* a coin," he said. "It *is* what a coin is like."

Eve watched him, her interest waning. She produced a limp cigarette. "I can always tell when a person doesn't quite *get* travel," she said, her thumb hovering, undecided, above the lighter's little wheel. "They're more like symbols than people, and yet their fright makes them seem so alive!"

The Wager

Two friends argued in their small hotel room in the city to which they had traveled at the insistence of one of them, who was named Greg. The other, Tom, had not wanted to go on the trip, but Greg, who had no children, had made traveling together a condition of their friendship, and Tom had come to accept their friendship as his only.

In the city to which the two friends had traveled, it was still possible to encounter new saints, and, at the time of their arrival, a fresh one had just evolved.

The new saint was a boy who, at the time of his birth, had been diagnosed with an incurable disease that would considerably foreshorten his life. For seven years, the boy had thrived in the murky atmosphere of his parents' grief—he had not been told that he was ill—until, at age eight, a cure was discovered.

But the boy, disoriented by the revelation of his illness, refused to be made better. He missed his parents' sadness, which had been for him a kind of thorny bush in which he'd been sweetly tangled, and he did not like their sudden exuberance, which bloomed deliriously and without end.

The boy's parents could not accept their son's refusal to be well—he was only a child, they told themselves—so they took him to court. But the city's constitution, though otherwise conservative, contained an amendment in support of children's rights, so the proceedings were futile and repugnant to everyone involved, especially the boy, who discovered, during his parents' testimony, that his existence had long served as the sole justification for their existence. If not for him, they would be lost.

The boy was so turned off by his parents' parasitical devotion that when he won the case—helped along by the culture's tacit support for extinction—he decided to emancipate himself from his parents' care, and when he had achieved that, too, his parents became suicides, and the boy was thrust into a truer emancipation than he'd ever dared to imagine.

From that time on, he'd lived in a triangular park bound by three pedestrian streets, spending his days in almost total silence beneath the single palm that grew there and his nights in a wooden crate covered by a bright blue tarp.

The city tried to step in more than once. They offered material aid—blankets, clothing, food—all of which the boy had declined, as was his right under the amendment. His refusal to accept even this diffuse, public parentage caught the eye of a local church, who, seeing that the boy had chosen something other than life, began the process of canonization.

THE ARGUMENT BETWEEN GREG AND TOM HAD NOTHING to do with the boy, though they had briefly discussed the strange case, which, they both agreed, could never have occurred in the cities where they lived. They had not lingered long on the topic so as not to have to wonder, together, whether the boy was truly a saint, as neither of them wanted, in the presence of the other, to make the difficult wager that would be required by such a conversation.

They were arguing, instead, about sleep. In their small hotel room, Greg couldn't do it. He sensed that Tom was not quite as tired as he was, which seemed to point toward Tom's incomplete identification with the friendship. In fact, since their arrival in the city, Tom had not seemed entirely amenable to many of Greg's views, though Greg could not prove that this was the case because Tom almost never disagreed with him.

Now it was late at night, and Greg was tired of denying the truth of his own perception. He could not sleep because Tom was awake, and Tom was awake because he did not love him.

He did not say as much to Tom. He explained, instead, that consciousness was contagious. While Tom was alert, Greg could not settle down, and, as Tom knew, Greg very much needed to settle down because he'd had a difficult day.

That morning, Greg had paid one of the city's public scribes to write a letter to his estranged father. Because this was an activity that many tourists undertook while on vacation in this particular city, Tom had performed support for the endeavor, though he knew it would likely require Greg to spend some damaging hours in the scribe's dark cell, where he would be asked to give a detailed account, at great cost to his personal equilibrium, of his father's failings, as well as the effect of those failings on Greg's career and his ability to see the good in others.

When Greg emerged from the cell, letter in hand, he told Tom, who had not thought of his own childhood for many years, that he did not intend to send the letter but instead to rework it and publish it under a pseudonym. Tom stared thoughtfully at the scribe's illegible scrawl before pointing out that this would go against the ancient terms Greg had agreed to when he'd engaged the scribe's services.

But Greg had dismissed this concern—the story was his, after all, it was his life, and his father was an awful person who deserved to be exposed. Besides, Greg did not actually live in the city, so he did not have to abide by its customs.

The scribe had overheard this conversation—the door of his cell had been constructed to amplify the noise of the street—and he emerged from his dark place to snatch the letter from Greg's hands.

The customs of this city were not municipal but universal, said the scribe, and the terms of the letter-writing agreement, once broken, could not be repaired. Now that Greg had indicated his intent, the letter and its contents—the rights to his entire childhood as he had described it—belonged to the city.

The scribe receded into his cell.

Greg lingered in the dark doorway. This certainly didn't seem fair, he said. It was *his* childhood, and he deserved to know just what exactly the city intended to do with it.

The scribe said nothing. He had learned, during their long interview, that silence was the favorite punishment of Greg's father, and his use of it now thrust Greg painfully into the past, from which cruelly imagined place, he began to beg the scribe, as he'd once begged his father, for a word, any word, just a sign that he was still living.

But the scribe wouldn't speak, and Greg was afraid to enter that dark place, not liking to go where he had not been enthusiastically invited.

At the threshold, his voice edging higher and higher, Greg tried to strike a bargain. He was beginning to accept that he'd done something awful, he said, something for which he was certainly deserving of a swift and total punishment. He would accept his fate, he swore he would, if the scribe would only speak to him again.

A crowd of tourists had begun to gather. Generally, Tom tried not to touch his friend, but now he took Greg by the arm and led him around the corner to a café. There he bought him a pastry, which Greg could not bring himself to eat, though the fact of Tom's having spent money on him did have a mildly restorative effect.

Greg had spent the rest of the day marveling over the scribe's consummate cruelty, admiring it, cherishing it even, until he remembered, over a light supper of bread and sardines, that he was no longer in sole ownership of his youth, which caused his mood to dip. The more he talked about his experience, the more universal it began to seem. In the end, he managed to extend the incident into a truism—people *would* use your childhood against you, he concluded, even if you were a child, or just like one.

Now Greg sighed in his single bed. As Tom must surely understand, Greg whined, he was really very tired from realizing the truth of things, and their hotel room was so small, he simply could not disentangle energetically from his friend— he was sorry about it, really he was, but Tom would have to go to sleep. Yes, even if he wasn't sleepy. He couldn't just lie there in the dark, thinking his separate thoughts. They were on vacation *together*, after all, and it was time for Tom to come through.

Tom sat up and put on his shoes.

He was going for a walk, he said. He would be back soon.

Greg, whose belief in Tom's faithfulness was such that he could not register his friend's failure to comply, went on cajoling Tom for some time after he'd left, unintentionally revealing many cynical beliefs about human nature that he had evolved privately and recently, though they had their origin in the distant past, perhaps even from before he was born.

THE BLUE TARP CRINKLED AS TOM LIFTED IT. FROM IN-
side the crate flowed a fetid smell of afterbirth.

The new saint was sleeping. On the ground, near the boy's
shapely feet, were an open envelope and a few empty milk car-
tons. His face was tucked away from Tom, into the nest that his
thin arms made. His back heaved with labored breath.

Tom knelt. The tarp dropped shut behind him. He removed the slim fold of paper from the open envelope. It was
a letter—a formal notification of the decision to canonize the
boy—in the squared and faultless handwriting of the church's
private scribe.

This, they wrote, would be their only communication. The
canonization process did not require his participation or consent, and once begun, it could not be interrupted, but they did
want to let him know it was going to happen. He should not
try to contact them. If he wrote back to this address, his letter
would not be received, but their thoughts were always with
him, even if they intended never to speak to him again.

On the street, a woman shrieked, *You power devil!*

The new saint rolled over. His white shirt was smeared with
blood and something darker. He reached for Tom's arm and
weakly squeezed it, his expression apologetic but determined.

He was so glad to see him, the boy said. He had a problem—his shirt was too tight. It was constricting him, making
it hard to breathe, and it seemed to be cutting into him, too,
cutting into him like a wire, though it was so soft. He was
bleeding from the tightness of his soft shirt, but he couldn't remove it himself because a stiffness had set in, from sleeping on
the ground probably, and he couldn't raise his arms.

Tom could see that the blood was coming not from the
boy's chest but from his full lips. It was dropping periodically
onto the front of his loose, white shirt. The problem was inter-
nal. The disease, thought Tom, was running its course.

Tom stared at the boy, who looked familiar, friendly even, though Tom didn't have any friends but Greg.

The boy smiled. He closed his eyes and coughed, and the blood that came forth was fine. It hung in the air for a moment, settling on Tom's right breast like a shield.

Tom touched the boy's foot, which was gray and cold.

Someone would come, Tom said to the boy. There would be someone on the way. Someone who wanted to be there.

The boy nodded. That was good, he said. He didn't like to ask for help. He knew people didn't really like to give it.

Tom lowered the tarp between them.

Buoyed by a newfound sense of freedom, Tom left the triangular park and began to explore the city. He lingered outside of a crowded bar, looking up and down the street as if he were expecting someone. When a young couple emerged, he followed them closely, observing the subtle choreography of the argument they were having.

The man was upset because his right foot had begun to hurt. This was the very foot that had begun to hurt his father toward the end of his life. Did this mean that he, too, was about to die?

The woman sighed. This was her vacation, too. Couldn't they break from the old routines? Couldn't they skip the unanswerables? She just wanted to have a good time, maybe eat something sweet. Ice cream, that's what she wanted. Wasn't there a place somewhere around here? Hadn't they passed a big cone with a face just a few minutes ago? If his feet hurt, he should just go back to the hotel. She would probably have a better time by herself. It was hard to think straight, with all his worrying.

It was not his *feet* that hurt, he insisted. It was his *foot*. His *right* foot.

Tom thought about something he knew, though he did not know where he'd learned it: *The right foot of the child is the brain of the father's corpse.*

Tom tapped the woman on the shoulder. The right food of the child, he said to her, is the brain of the father's corpse.

The couple looked at Tom with alarm. They linked arms and turned away. Brought together by his aberrant behavior, they delivered themselves into the protective light of an ice cream parlor, where Tom could not follow.

He looked back toward the park and saw a crowd streaming toward him, wracked by some collective emotion. From a distance, they appeared to be crying, but as they came nearer, it seemed possible that they were laughing instead.

It would have been easy enough to ask. Something had happened, something terrible or ridiculous or both, but it wouldn't do to dig deep. After all, he was only visiting the city. It was his duty to stay on the surface of things.

He decided to take a different route back to the hotel. At times, he felt a trailing presence, someone small and exacting at his feet, but every time he turned around, he found that he was still alone.

It was early morning in their small hotel room, and Greg was in bed. He had accepted, sometime in the night, that Tom was not coming back.

To keep from thinking about it, he was reading a memoir written by someone he knew. In the book, his acquaintance had written a sentence that began, *When I am rich and famous…*, but he knew that this acquaintance was already very rich.

Greg wondered: Was this how it worked? Did you have to assert that you were neither rich nor famous when in fact you were very much one of them, so that the other would come true?

Other than this troubling contrivance, Greg enjoyed reading the book, whose subtleties he ignored, preferring to map onto it a meaning that confirmed his own strong feelings about those who refused the true support of the only ones who really loved them.

A Waste of Life

I REFUSED TO TIPTOE AROUND IN OUR CO-ED HOSTEL room because it was the middle of the day and Joachim had been sleeping for at least fourteen hours, which, for a living person, is a restorative amount of time. Add to that, despite the fact that I had arrived at the hostel two days ago, I had not yet seen him awake, so to me he was simply the suggestion of a man and nothing more.

I sat down heavily on my bottom bunk (he was on top). I tooted my little wooden flute. But Maureen, who had seen Joachim awake, having encountered him in the common room prior to my arrival, was trying not to make any noise.

He's sleeping, she said.

So what? I was awake!

While Joachim was awake, Maureen had learned the following about him: He was on vacation by himself. From America. San Francisco, to be exact. In his youth, he had wanted to be an artist. But art school had been a joke, an absolute laugh (between friends, no less!), so he decided he would be an engineer. *A mastermind,* he said to himself, *that's what I'll be. Nothing funny about that.* (Nothing friendly either.) But, as it turned out, he had more natural feeling than could be expressed by a bridge, or an oil rig, or a skyscraper, so he had settled, at last, on the profession of nurse. He would become a nurse, and as a nurse he would really and truly and finally help. (Behind all this, he insisted, was his great and real love of people.)

But first, he deserved a vacation.

We told each other this story repeatedly, Maureen and me. We marveled at it, turned it over on our tongues: Joachim had traveled to a foreign country as a last hurrah, before beginning to help. He meant to have a very good time, if only he could just wake up!

Joachim, in their single interview, had also asked about Maureen's life—it was the polite thing to do between Americans—and she had made the fatal mistake of admitting that she was a writer, in school for writing. *But what,* asked Joachim, who really should have been asleep, *will you do with that?* (His decision, regarding art school, had been final.)

Thank God I had given all that up!

Maureen, though, could not forget what she had learned about Joachim, and she could not forgive him his question (What *would* she do?), but she was and has always been beholden to the object of a sleeping man, so she tried to make very little noise.

I slammed my suitcase shut. Maureen winced. She pointed to the top bunk, to Joachim's body laying supine in jeans (incredibly, he had dressed for the day). *Shhh!*

She was talking to me!

In my view, Joachim's sleep was not a moral failing, but a declaration regarding space—he was like: I've got a right to it. Which is why I did what I did next, which was flap my hot pink parasol open and shut, open and shut, in a display of three-dimensional dominance. If he did not already know, I would show him, by my flapping, that the living mattered more than the dead!

But to Maureen, who moved so quietly about the room, who tipped and toed her feather-light body back and forth between her backpack and her bunk, Joachim was rotten. A bad apple. She knew it by his sleep, by the way his sleep made her move. And as if to confirm it, his computer was always in bed with him. It could, in a way, be said to be breathing—you know that little light? That purity? It was an Apple that owned his pulse. There it was. And there.

So I wasn't worried about Joachim. Not for a second. He had his breath, and his nursing plans. And I had other concerns. Like: What color was my bruise today? And: Why did Maureen want to be so quiet in the hostel room that we shared with Joachim? *Go on*, I said to her. *You don't need his permission. You're awake, so make a little noise!*

(Still, I know how it can be. You get the feeling, sometimes, that you might have given birth and forgotten all about it. Could *he* be my baby? Could *he*? Even if you sustain, by the teeth of that man, a big old bruise, it's often safest to assume that you're his mother.)

In the end, because we could not decide either to make noise or to be quiet, Joachim was always with us. He could not be escaped, though he was not in pursuit (he wasn't moving).

We could be sitting on the terrace, and Maureen would say: *What a waste.* We could be sipping our café con leche or our Frenadol con agua, the sun on our big and little necks, and Maureen would say: *Joachim, what a waste of life.*

But who knows what it's like to be dead?

It really got to be a problem. We could be up on a rampart or down on the empty beach or at a café, wrist-deep in a hot pile of shrimp. We could be feeling all around in a hot pile of shrimp, having a perfectly good time doing almost nothing, doing that which was very close to sleeping while being awake, and Maureen would jump to her feet: *We've got to be doing something! We cannot be like Joachim!*

But Joachim was fast asleep, and my feet were beginning to ache from all that walking.

It was one of those times when Maureen, not wanting to be Joachim, was making us march around town in the hot pre-night despite our already very long day, when we came upon the hole.

The hole was historic. It had been dug during medieval times by a hundred women, ninety-eight of whom had died during their labor, by order of Queen Ferdinand, who had tired of the king's relentless pursuit of her and decided to show him, in concrete terms, just how big she would get if she allowed him to do as he pleased. So it was a really huge hole, and many women had died down inside of it, gripping shovels like flotation devices, vomiting dirt, all because, as the placard read: *The king never learned to divert himself.*

The hole was the size of a building underground. It was possible to walk right over it on a giant sheet of plexiglass, and so we did. And we did look down. And what we saw, oh so cozy on the packed dirt floor, tucked hermetically away from life inside of that monumental absence, was a sleeping man. Was he breathing? You guessed it. He was fogging up the plexiglass. He was greenhouse gassing himself into a magnitude of rest that surpassed, even, Joachim's. I'm not afraid to call it death. (If I sound bitter it's because such sleep is unavailable to me.)

We stood there for quite a long time. Just as night fell, a light came on at the bottom of the hole. Our up-skirts were celestialized. We were standing on the surface of our suburban childhoods as our fathers had always dreamed they would never be. The sleeping man, of course, was not bothered by the flood of light.

Shhh! Maureen said as I stomped on the sturdy plexiglass.

You shouldn't do that, said the disembodied voice of some nearby tourist. *Men need their sleep, too.*

And I could not, in that bright moment, disagree.

Mumbai

W_HEN HE COULD NO LONGER STAND HER DREAM_ chatter—*there were two trucks, one containing the ingredients for a circus, the other the ingredients for war, but I was just one person sloshing around in a giant abalone shell, so what could I do?*—he left Nancy on the hotel roof with the chef from Mumbai. He regretted, only, that he would not hear the story of the shipwreck that the chef had promised to tell—*I'll say that I was holding a basketball when we went down. I'll tempt you with that.*

He walked up in the night, past the central church, down the alley redolent with smoked paprika, and through the neighborhood of scaling stone, stopping at the very top of the ridge to drink at the town trough. To the left was the warm sink of the crowded town, to the right the long beach. The living boats. Every shrimp on fire. Every foot. Every fist raised and full of fish, dripping with the fluids of fish. And the construction site where inside was the perfect seat of moss, where he'd hoisted Nancy's body onto his and bounced her around on his lap without thinking of what would happen to the jade-green moss beneath him. It had ended as a stain on Nancy's knees, not a breathing color anymore, not a color bursting with air.

Bending down to the trough was difficult. His exertions had cost him. The water flowed thick from a hole in the wall and sometimes bubbled out as if the giant mouth of the place were pushing. He took a sip. On his knees he was nearer to the lemons. He picked one up and it was her fine round head. He thought: *See, Isa, lemons. If you were here with me, we'd be in the basket. Come to the coast. Meet me, after all.*

Fine and round and pink was the body he'd left behind. Impossible to stain. Useful. Like a ladder or a hutch. Or a bowl. What could cook there, what could brew, in the firm middle of her.

He wiped his mouth and looked around. Two old men raised their knees, removed their left shoes, and sunk their left feet into the water inside the trough. They held on to each other for support, arms across backs. Together they cooled their feet, and when they were done and dry, they left each other without a word. Vacation was a yawning, what did it matter who sank by his side. Just a body after all, pink or not. Just a weight.

Nancy on the roof. Breathless on the roof. Nancy upside down. Nancy, a lake of eels. Isa, a ladder or a hutch. It wasn't too late to feel it tonight. He started down the road to the long beach.

On his way, he met no one. The sidewalk disappeared, and small stacked homes gave way to elaborate tricky ones that would not admit to a door. Beside the road was a thin moat through which water ran swifter than sense, and he tried to run along with it, faster and faster, his knees crying out, until the stream disappeared abruptly beneath concrete. A scooter buzzed by and a soft hand reached out, stealing his glasses off his face. The hand yelled, "Aieeee," and disappeared. He was in the road. The middle of it. A dark road.

He followed what he thought was the edge, the safest place, until he saw the flames and the long string of light that meant he'd arrived at the beach. His foot touched the sponge of wood. The boardwalk was full tonight. He moved through a crowd of soft, smudged faces. He saw no personal landscape. This was tone without texture. Beige-brown. The color of slinking through the arcade that stretched between his competing desires.

A long skirt wound around his ankle. He stopped and shook it off. He sat at a table outside of a café, and felt the squirm of Nancy calling him back to the hotel—*you wouldn't believe what I've found to be true of men living in the north, it's shocking, I've found my shoes on fire, a whole pile of them, my pillows drained, my curios crushed, it's daddy desire up there, guilty, I had to start calling myself Nancy—*

"This table is not empty," said a man.

He turned to the not-face, the beige-brown, and nodded. "Excuse me. I didn't see you there."

"You're welcome to stay."

"I will, if you don't mind."

"Chato," said the man.

"Chato, I've lost my glasses."

"A shame. But there are only so many roads home," said Chato.

"I'm on vacation."

"Funny. You have what they call *the tone*."

"So I've heard."

He smelled what he thought was a woman coming close. He did not turn around.

The waiter brought a bottle of wine and a bowl of round nuts. He couldn't see to pour himself a glass but rolled the nuts, spiced and charred, into his mouth and held out his arm. Chato filled a glass and slipped it into his waiting hand. He took a sip of what he'd been given.

"You're here for the living boats?" said Chato.

"No, I don't think so."

"They were marvelous, once, before the boardwalk. I remember the first. Nature proved to me that she could play, that she could be a scientist too. But back then they were wild. Tricky. Not like the big blimps you see today, all lined up for the tourist's chum. The whole thing is so indelicate."

"You don't like the beach."

Chato shuddered. "No. I come for the women."

He took a longer sip of wine and closed his eyes and heard the distant whir that was the call of the living boats, so close to the real thing, but mournful, quickening.

Chato leaned over the bowl of nuts and the top of his head came into focus. A thin run of bowing hair, a silvery grass at dawn. "Are you alone?" he asked.

"For the night."

"You left her at the hotel?"

"She wouldn't come."

"Is that so?"

He could not see the details of Chato's expression, but he could see that he had turned around in his seat as if to search for someone else, someone truer, and he was moved to keep him at the table just a little longer, just until he could finish the wine and the nuts and prepare himself for the dark walk home to the hotel, where he would slip into bed and find, or not find, the body he'd left behind.

"Well, there is no her. Not really," he said.

Chato relaxed into his chair. "There never is," he said. "Or, there was once a girl we loved, one girl, but we couldn't keep her, so we grew tentacles and attached ourselves to many fairer lives. Have I got you buried?"

"No, not me. There was never one for me."

Chato sighed and his sharp breath crushed any remaining primness between them. "There was for me," he said. "There was one."

Chato slid the bowl of nuts across the table. The string of light took shape against the darkening night. It was getting late. The boats had gone to bed many miles from the beach. The tourists were drinking, they had not washed. The spirits of fish, mangled, rebuking, floated alongside them, swishing their deadly scent.

He could not stand it. He took one last nut and raised it to his mouth and saw that his fingertips were pink and he wiggled the tiny pink circles in the air in front of his face and thought: just heads, they are only heads.

Chato got up. "Marrow dust," he said. "Marrow from the long bones. The sweetest middle."

He got up too and, first wiping the marrow on his pants, extended a hand to Chato. "Good to meet you," he said.

Chato took his arm. "Walk with me," he said. "I can't let this night go."

They moved together across the sponge of wood, through the crowd, the beige-brown smear. He held on tight. Chato's arm was thick as Isa's, packed firm around the bone. The air, or the crowd, squeezed the two men together. He let the silver brush his cheek, he smelled the salty string of sea.

"What can you see?" asked Chato.

"Very little."

"Shape?"

"Yes and color and tone."

"That's fine," said Chato. "I'll get you halfway home. I've got an appointment at the trough."

"It's pleasant, actually. I'm enjoying myself."

"Are you?"

"Yes."

"We'll go a little longer then."

At the edge of the boardwalk, he hesitated. Chato patted him on the back. "Just a little step down," he said. "Hop it. Don't be afraid."

Late at night, Isa, at the top of a hill he refused to climb, waved her mittened hand. Pink and round and risen, her head. High and light. Cream of the creamy mountain. She waved and waved and behind her came the curtain of green, the infolding flame, and it shone on the hill of snow, becoming pink, borrowing pink from her pink, draining her, it was taking her away, but he must not let it! He ran a short way up the mountainside, and she shook her head to make him stop and slid down the snowy slope on her sturdy butt and whispered: *Be still or you'll scare her away. She is only a glow.*

He hopped onto the sand. Chato held his elbow. "A delicate hop for a careful man," he said.

Slow going through the sand. Small suns setting down. Chato gave a squeeze.

"Bonfires," said Chato. "Youth!"

They moved from the dark sand to the darker street.

"It was somewhere here, where my glasses went."

"I hope you've let them go," Chato said.

"I have."

Together they climbed to the top of the ridge. Chato dipped the cup of his hand into the trough and drank and offered the cup to him and he drank too.

"You can't see them," said Chato, "but they're visible to me. The living boats are sleeping. Their breath makes a little cloud. It hangs there. I see it now."

He stared into the formless night and saw no distance. He reached behind him and felt a bench and sat down.

Chato sat beside him and rubbed his knee. "Good," he said. "Just a little longer."

"Nancy won't be waiting," he said.

"No, she won't," said Chato.

Nancy.

Chato scraped his feet over the ground. "The cloud of the sleep of the living boats always puts me in mind of her," he said. "The girl. There was one for me."

"Oh?" he said, though he was not interested. He reached up to adjust the glasses that were not there and was surprised by the hollow dips of his eyes.

"Catalina," Chato continued. "I met her 30 years ago, when there was no boardwalk. Back then I sold lemons on the street. I'd heard news of the living boats, but I was up so late at the movies, every night at the movies. I couldn't be bothered to see for myself. I was exhausted, I know that now. I was sick.

"I met Catalina over lemons. She bought a bag. We liked each other immediately. She was demure, wore long woolen skirts that hung past her ankles, even in the summer, even to the beach.

"We started seeing each other. Mostly during the day. How can I put this? At first you could ride the living boats. There were a few years when we were pre-humane and a ride on the boats was pretty cheap. We went, Catalina and I, to the dock, we paid, and when she went to hop on the boat, when she pulled her long skirt up, the boat spooked and swam away, and she fell into the ocean. She went under for a moment and popped up butt-first. Her skirt was all around. She wore nothing underneath. She was bare. There's no excuse for what happened next—I pushed her down. With my boot, I pushed her back under the water. Do you know what it was like? Her bareness?"

"No." He sensed a change, the raising of the hackles of the ridge on which they stood.

Chato pointed down the path. A head, pink and round and risen, came toward them through the night. High and spooky, it drifted side to side. It had no body, no body at all. He looked away.

"It was just like that," said Chato. "Just like a pink balloon. Joyful. Just a little mischievous. And still I pushed it down."

The head came closer, and he could see that someone held it. A child. And the child was held by its parent, a mother. A pink balloon and a child and its mother.

"At that moment, my life was split," Chato said. "There was the time before The Push, and the time after." He gestured toward the child and its mother. "Here is my daughter," he said, "and here is my wife."

Chato took the pink balloon from his daughter. The two women walked ahead. Chato stood so still he disappeared. Only the balloon was there, the kind and simple head of the balloon, pink as ever, pink at night.

"Do you know when I think of her now there is never a face. I cannot remember her face. I'm what they call a baby praying at a grave, when I think of her." He shook his head.

"I'll be late if I don't go now. Nancy will wonder."

IN THE BLACK HALLWAY, HE COUNTED THE DOORS. HE scraped the key along the wood until it found its home in the knob. Nancy was asleep in the firm hotel bed. He brushed her dark hair off his pillow.

"You're back," she said. "You missed a wild night. The chef told his story."

"How did it end?"

Nancy flipped on the light and threw the sheets off her body.

"Well, he survived. He floated for 51 hours in the open water. It was his basketball! His basketball kept him alive. It was late at night. He couldn't sleep. He came up on the deck to shoot some hoops and get some air and the ship suddenly turned on its side. The rest drowned. All the rest."

"Listen, Nancy."

"And do you know what else he said?"

"Nancy."

"He said that he didn't feel anything for the ball. Not anything at all. Not grateful to it or thankful for its help. He said that to care for it, to love it, he would have had to think of it as a head. But he couldn't. He couldn't think of it as a head. And so he couldn't care. He couldn't get attached. The ball wasn't his friend. He just used it. He used it to stay alive, and when he was rescued he left it in the sea. We have to go to Mumbai. We have to go. He says it's full. The city is full but it keeps on growing anyway. Somehow it keeps on growing. He says it'll never stop. It's magic, he says, that way it doesn't explode."

Vacation

The sunlight was solid. She would not walk down to the sea because it had been flattened by the sunlight, and she could not determine its temperament from her spot in the chair by the pool.

The villa belonging to the gob factory was two-tiered. There was the long low adobe house and there was the pool. There was also the garden and the garden was everywhere. From the window of her room on the second tier she could touch the blades of a pepper tree whose roots were sunk deep in the lawn. At night, there were twinkling lights in the tree, but no one to turn them on. Her vacation slot had not coincided with the slot of any other worker.

For two whole weeks, she would not assist in the making of gobs. Her hands were clean and dry now. She spent some time floating in the pool. Otherwise, she walked through the garden, squinting without pants. Twice a day she stood at the long metal table in the kitchen and ate a tomato sandwich.

At night she lay on top of the sheets in the single outfit she'd brought. She kept the window wide open. It cooled off around two a.m., and it was also around this time that she could no longer keep the gobs at bay. They would visit her: red and green and gray. They would lump around the twinkling of the lights, pretending to be the fruit of the pepper tree.

In the morning she thought: But aren't I alone? There was a pair of straw shoes on the patio. There were tangerine rinds in the garden and a pile of white clothing by the pool. She stood by her chair and looked up at the long low house. The windows worked like mirrors against the sunlight. They reflected the white sky, which was more solid even than the solid sun and painful to look at even when she didn't use her eyes.

All day long, she made sure to wear pants. She used fewer tomatoes. She kept a seed between her teeth that she intended to remove at first sight. There was a moment near the milk vetch when its red-green pod rattled off and she thought someone was coming down the path but it was nothing and no one was coming.

That night when the gob-time came she lay like normal on top of the sheets. Her feet were clean, which had taken some work. The clean and shining faces of her feet were facing the open window and, in the moment before the gobs materialized, the twinkling lights were thin and white and her relationship to lying down was simple. But when the gobs took the light (red and green and gray) she experienced a metaphysical lengthening of arm. She was not merely noting the presence of the gobs. She was working on them. She was shaping them around the glow. But when she brought her hands up to her face, they were clean and dry.

She heard a distant splash. She snuck up to the open window on her belly. The pool was dark but there was someone in it. His butt was a buoyant pearl that had surfaced to court the moon.

She watched for a long time. She had a desperate appetite for swimming and so did he—but he was the one in the water. The twinkling lights impressed themselves upon her. She went down the hall and saw them twinkling and mixing in the toilet. So she decided that she would go. She would join him. But when she came back to the window, he was gone. The gobs stayed with her when she closed her eyes. Even in her dreams—gobs. It would be gobs.

The next morning passed without incident. She thought again about getting down to the sea but she could not find her sunglasses. She smoothed the gravel path with the ornamental rake and dared to touch the bright yellow flower of the prickly pear. At noon she attempted a nap. She lay on top of the sheets with dirty feet. And the pepper tree whispered: *Someone is coming*.

It could have been an hour. There was a sound at the door. She turned the knob to release the latch but she didn't pull. She felt a slight pressure from the other side and let the door open as wide as the pressure asked. She didn't look out. She stood back from the door and was looking at the door but not around it. His arm came into the room. It was lean and dark-haired and strong. It moved around like a periscope. An impossible twist of the wrist. The suggestion of a ball bearing and a rubber band. Then it disappeared. The door closed. She fell back on the bed. She was warm to the neck but no higher.

Later that day she stood near the buckwheat in bloom and paid homage to the long-gone seed head by shaping an imagined gob in its image. A gob the color of dried blood. A gob the shape of the plum inside a sparrow's skull. There were all the bursts of white that were not the gob that she was shaping behind her eyes. There were the hundred heads of white that she was shaping. And above the buckwheat spray was the head of that someone she had been expecting, that someone who had finally come.

"Will you help me?" he said. His shoulders sloped down. He had no shirt on. His body was a series of narrowing widths that ended in sinewy ankle. In the solid sun he was colored sand. She knew he would be hot to the touch.

She nodded.

He looked relieved. "I want to tidy some plants."

He walked off down the gravel path. He was moving toward the flattened sea. She followed, squinting.

They came to a short rocky slope. The path down the cliff was just beyond. There were ten large succulents growing there in the dirt. Their lances were juicy with spikes. They were jagged green rosettes. And around the base of each rosette were some dead and shriveled parts. They looked like they would live forever, dead.

He crouched. He was standing on the slope, one foot up and one foot down. He pointed at the juicy lances and then at the dessicated offshoots that fanned out around the base of the succulents. "These have to go," he said.

She started to pull.

He watched her critically. "You're being too delicate. Stop acting like you're at the factory."

Her face burned with shame. He was standing in front of the sun. His head was a deep black oval that was fat.

"Listen," he said. "I don't have a mother or a father. I don't even have a friend. I was a countertenor. I was a nurse in the last hospital standing. I was dragging corpses from the river. There is no one left but you."

"And you," she said. He came closer and there was no sun. She stood in his gray shade and looked at him. His face was glistening with sweat or with oil.

He frowned. "We have to do this without our clothes on in order not to get infected. Our clothes are filthy. If we get jabbed through our clothes, we risk getting pierced by disease."

He disrobed quickly.

"Okay," she said. She lifted her arms and looked up. He helped her off with her shirt and then removed her shoes. She did the rest herself and got down to work.

The succulents jiggled as she pulled and so did her body. It was hard to break off the dead parts. Her knees were scraped bloody by the rocks. Meanwhile she watched him work. He did everything in frantic bursts like a lizard surprised. He worked with his back toward her. His butt was solid in the sunlight. His penis dangled shyly as he crouched, never touching the dirt. But almost.

It could have been an entire day. Together they made quite a pile. The sun sat at a devastating angle. The reflection off the sea hit like a heavy blade on the bridge of her nose.

When they had finished, he surveyed their work. "Good," he said. "I like a clean base. How do you feel?"

She wasn't sure. She ground some dirt between her teeth. It had snuck in, she could not get it out. He gathered his clothing—and hers—and started back toward the villa.

"Meet me for dinner," he shouted from up ahead. "We'll eat under the arbor."

By the time she got to the pool he had dipped and disappeared. His footprints had had time to shrink in the sun. In the shower she remembered that he had her only clothes. She lay down naked on top of the sheets with wet hair. The sun had hardly set when the twinkling lights came on. The gobs came right away and her arms defied her—she had not intended to work anymore—and she shaped the red and green and gray with skill and speed in his likeness.

He was sitting at the table. There was one bulb dangling from the arbor. Two moths bopped the bulb and the grapes gobbed all around.

She came naked. There was no other choice. He was wearing a button-down shirt and loose gray trousers.

"You have my clothes," she said.

"It's good to have some time off." He plucked a chalky grape that housed an inner light.

She sat down. The chair was made of reeds that stuck her.

"I guess," she said.

"This still counts as time off because when I'm here, I choose to work. I work only when I want to work, which makes all the difference."

"I haven't done anything since I got here. Nothing I really want to do, yet."

"You will," he said. His face was kind but distant. He filled her plate.

They ate tuna in oil. There were spoonfuls of capers. She held fish skin in her teeth. He crushed a tomato in his hand and flung it onto the grass. They laughed.

Later, they swam. He took off his clothes and did laps. She bobbed in his wake. Twice she experienced an uncontrollable lengthening of arm, but he did not seem to feel her in the waves.

He helped her out of the pool and into a warm towel. She shrugged it off and was naked again. She took his neck in her hands and pulled his face to hers. She pried his lips apart with her tongue and inside him found an olive and took it and chewed.

"There you go," he said and gently removed her. His penis was erect. His balls were glaucous and high and tight and in perfect imitation of gobs. She knew by looking at them that her vacation had passed her by.

The next morning, she found a form letter on the floor. It had been slipped beneath her door in the night.

Dear Sirs, it began,

I am writing to express my deepest gratitude for the use of the company villa. Vacation allowed me to... And here was a fill-in-the-blanks.

Signed,
Slot C Worker

She ate a tomato sandwich. She spilled a lake of seeds on the letter and wiped it away with the back of her hand. She took the letter with her and sat by the pool for hours. She slunk past the arbor where the table was still set. There were golden-green flies above the slick and shining scraps of food. She circled the scene of their eating and sat down on the reeded chair to get poked.

Dear Sirs,

I am writing to express my deepest gratitude for the use of the company villa. Vacation allowed me to bodily experience the gob, who kept me at arm's length. So I have you to thank for showing me what is a gob and how feels a gob (and how real) and how very gob I am.

Signed,
Slot C Worker

Her bare skin stung and stretched. She stood up. She kept on standing up. Higher and higher. An olive on her tongue. Her legs around his neck. Her fingers gripping his hair. She was riding on his shoulders with his head between her hands. She aimed him toward the flattened sea and squeezed.

The Guest

I WENT TO SPAIN BECAUSE I WAS NEEDED AT THE WED-
ding. It was necessary that I be there in order to be disinvited,
at the last minute, from one wedding-related event, thereby de-
lineating the exact boundary of the American groom's net of
intimacy. (The limit was me; the bride was Spanish.)

The event was a formal dinner held by the groom's family
in order to honor those intrepid and dedicated out-of-town
guests who had come all the way from America to celebrate.
That was fine. I was American, but I didn't want to be honored,
not by him, and besides I had not really been invited to the
wedding in the first place. I had kind of just shown up.

I was disinvited from the dinner in a text message that was
sent by someone other than the groom, which was necessary
because the groom did not have my phone number anymore.

I'm really annoyed to have to be the one to tell you this, texted this
person, who, being the size of a woman or smaller, had earned a
spot in the groom's expatriotism, *but it's a really small restaurant,*

and there just isn't room for one more. But he's super happy that you're coming to the wedding. Really. He says it's been too long…

On the night of the dinner, I went for a walk. I wandered down many alleys—I was a stranger to the city, despite my universal attitude—until I ended up right outside the window of the very restaurant in which the dinner was taking place. (A coincidence. I had not been allowed to know the address.)

The window was glowing with goodness, and in it was neatly framed the tan and handsome face of the groom. He was addressing his guests. Oh, how he was loving on those out-of-sight, out-of-town guests—you could tell by his dimples, and the regal purse of his lips. That winning smile! He would have charmed me if I had been, in his purview, a woman, but instead I am big and tall and secretly dumb, and I have no respect for facts or the people who wield them.

Technically, our eyes did meet—we were like two gowned queens swishing past—but in the field of erasing me, the groom was an expert. Plus it was necessary for him to behave as if I were not outside in the dark alley. (Nobody likes to admit the limits of his intimacy, but a limit is required, for coziness. That's what marriage is all about!)

So there was the groom. His head. In the window. My big body was all that he could have seen, but he managed to look right through me—he had that most untrustworthy of masculine traits: self-control—though the fact of having to ignore me did make him pause, briefly, in that life-giving speech, which I could not properly hear (the dinner was loud; I was very much outside). Yes, for a moment, he did falter in his unrestrained praise of his guests, who had been invited, who had burned many tons of fuel to arrive in that cozy restaurant, and it seemed, for a moment, like he might lose it all the way—his groomness, that is—because of me.

So I decided to lose it first. I could, in my position, afford to. I placed my injured hand on the stone sill of the little window (there was no pane; the restaurant was Spanish). A child, inside and invited, noticed it lying there. She poked my poor hand, but it didn't hurt. I couldn't feel it. It wasn't, really, alive anymore. It was a blue-black bag of bones from which my swollen fingers hung.

The child, her eyes big and weird, looked out at me and asked: *What happened?*

Well, I answered, *it was something I'd wanted done to me, for a very long time, without knowing that I wanted it.*

The child stared. She squeezed my soft fingers incredulously.

It was a rather benign type of sacrifice, to show the groom what had become of me. And he did see it, there on the windowsill. It pleased him to no end what my hand seemed to prove—I would never arrive. I would never come in to join the rest. Not now. Not anymore. The disinvitation of me was total.

The groom made a full recovery, thanks to me. He regained, by my apparent absence, his grooming abilities. He opened his mouth wide and laughed—but not, it appeared to the guests, because of me. No, never because of me! (He would never admit me as inspiration.) He laughed because, so far as they could tell, he had made a joke—a joke that I could not hear over the din of his extremely well-attended event. His joke landed well. It always did. He was so popular.

You should write that down, said someone shrill, someone whose insider enthusiasm was great enough to reach the alley. *You should save that for later. If you want to be an artist you have to always be taking notes… you have to always have a notebook, and a pen… that's how you know someone's really serious about the whole thing… when they're scribbling away in the middle of a dinner party… in the middle of life! You might think nothing interesting's going on, but an artist—he's receiving all the time!*

I took my hand from the windowsill. The child began to cry, and I walked on.

At the end of the block, the alley opened onto a courtyard festooned with garlands of moon-muted flowers: A festival was happening in the city. It was that time of night, and the streetlights had been turned off to make it easier to see the projection of a famous painting onto the courtyard wall. I'll never forget it, because there it was: *Las Moscas*, painted in the year 1981 by the great Spanish artist Josefa Velásquez, who at the height of her fame and attractiveness (age 47), refused to relinquish her celibacy despite nearly drowning under wave after wave of desirable suitor-patrons. It wasn't easy, but she died poor and alone, that beneficent paintress. The muses never ceased to bless her, even after she refused to work. Yes, long after she was sunk in her grave… she had *ideas*. They swarmed her, you see. That's the plot!

But what am I after? You know the painting. Still, you cannot know the scene.

It was like this: In the foreground was La Mosquita, the toddler pre-wife, surrounded by her court of many maids, two invalids, and a no-tailed cat. She shimmered on the courtyard wall in her pearly ding-dong dress while I stood anonymously immersed in the hysterical happiness of the crowd, looking up at her. The middle ground was nothing; it was not there. And in the background was a narrow mirror, reflecting the artist herself, most elegantly disguised as a man.

I spun around to catch a glimpse. Through the crowd of festivalgoers, plus some other guests who had escaped, I saw the artist at her easel. She was dressed in black, her hair appropriately shorn. Her right foot, propped up on a stool, was a type of threat. Soon she would exit the frame. *In terms of this projection, her bent knee seemed to say, I would much rather not be here.*

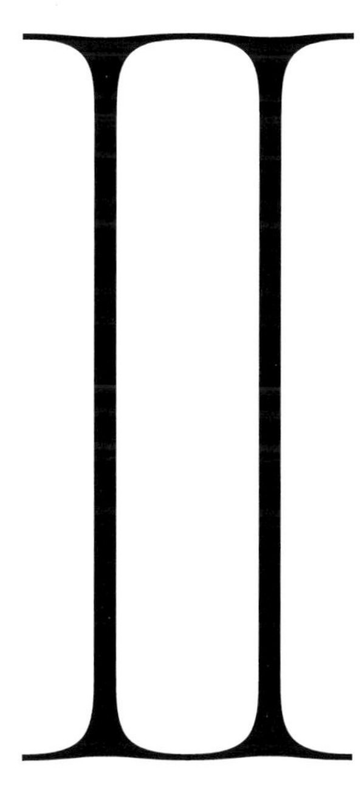

The Pale Pig

With relief, Mr. Pop saw that the paddock was empty. They had not left the body to rot. He walked up to the door of the big red house at the base of the mountain and pressed the bell. He waited, the whir and the whip of propellers sounding above. Miss Lister came to the door, holding roots in her big square hands. Clods of dirt slipped free and burst on the porch.

"Watch your shoes, Mr. P," she said. "I'm dropping bombs. Kiki is upstairs. Is she asleep? Could be, it's been quiet all morning. It's been quiet all week. The accident affected her! She's a real girl, it turns out. In some ways. Or at least she's had a shock."

Mr. Pop pressed his chin to his chest then thrust it up into the air, which was a movement he had learned meant yes.

Miss Lister shook her head. "You'll always be a stranger to me, Mr. P. You'll always confound me. Still, I sure am glad you're here. Will it bother you to work with Kiki in the kitchen today? I'm shaving roots in Mother's study. Got to get them free, got to have the TV to do it."

He shook his head no. High above, a metallic hiccup interrupted the whir and the whip. Miss Lister joined him on the porch. Together they looked up at the sky. A helicopter swayed and lurched on its way to the mountain. The architectural column that hung from its undercarriage wagged from side to side. Like a finger, the column said: No no no.

He thought he could see, in the helicopter's cabin, some pale creature at the controls. Oh, he thought. Oh! And though his knees were shaking, he found himself reaching up, reaching out—what was this? He was calling that paleness in.

The propellers stopped, the helicopter dropped straight down. Miss Lister tossed her roots. "Hey," she screamed. "Hey!" She ran toward the falling machine, her legs impeded by the vicious flapping of her long skirt and her heavy work-woman's shoes. Mr. Pop, his fingers fluttering over his throat, steeled himself for what was coming. But when the helicopter achieved its maximum nearness to the ground, he saw quite clearly who the pilot was—a heavily helmeted man, waving, cheerfully, hello. And then, as if the sudden drop had been nothing but a demonstration of the pilot's skill, the propellers sprang to life and whirled around again, at once invisible in their speed. The helicopter, its column tamed and hanging straight, went on its way up the mountainside.

Mr. Pop stepped off the porch and stared at his feet. He stood delirious before the landscape that he'd come to know so well. He saw the ice growing up from the dirt, the browning of the grass. The ascendance of the callous season.

Miss Lister came back toward the house, kicking her skirt out in front of her. The smooth edge of her right eye was raw and red. "What kind of work is tree replacement?" she said. "I hate that work. I don't see how it's possible, and you can bet nobody'll ever bother to explain it to me—not that I'd want to know! Trees replaced are not trees. Columns are columns no matter what. Have you been up there, Mr. P?"

"Yes," he said, avoiding her big honest eye. "I saw nothing living."

"So the forest is going temple," said Miss Lister, gathering her roots close. "It's what the people want! And what do you or I know about that?"

She squeezed his shoulder with her powerful hand. "Now, Kiki's got to get up. She can't coast along on her shock forever. A horse is a horse. We are all vulnerable to injury. Better she learn that lesson than go around thinking we are all so solid. I'll rustle her up."

Mr. Pop went inside and stood in the entryway, but Kiki did not come down. Downstairs he was the only one. Father, were he around—well, such a man would not stay hidden for long.

In the quiet of waiting, Mr. Pop performed a calisthenic routine he had learned in the army decades ago. Faster and faster, he made the familiar movements in order, his body readily complying, until a swift bend forward caused his head to swell with blood and a rush of cloudy drool to slip unbidden from his mouth to the floor.

He stood, chastened, on the spot of drool. He could leave if he wanted to. Father was not around. But here came Kiki, down the stairs. She was in the middle of pulling on her bloating sleeves—he had never, in their year together, seen her free of those glossy lengths. Her bare arms were massive. At intervals they seemed to be bound tightly by strings that vanished into her flesh, so fiercely was her skin trying to rein things in.

She had not brought her books down from her room. Her hair had not been brushed, not for days.

"Pop," she said, "Pop Man. I'm not up to it today."

"Study time," he said. "If not the books, then the flashcards."

She frowned. "Maybe you're used to not getting what you want, but I'm a little girl. I don't have to suffer in silence. I don't feel good."

"Not so little," he said. "Grown up."

"Yes, little," she said. "Father says I am." She yawned and stretched, and a few inches of her stomach showed above the elastic of her pants. Across the pure white expanse of her skin was an angry line of red.

"Father says study," said Mr. Pop. "Father says time to start again. He says no interruption necessary."

"Father knows I'm upset," she said. "He says I should take it easy. Last night he came in very late and sat on the bed and said that Lump loves me, Lump is the greatest horse, Lump wasn't trying to kill herself. Lump is not like a mother. What happened was she got too excited that I was finally riding her and sometimes we like something so much that we can't stand it so we throw it away. I'm not mad at Lump, I just feel funny about her, that's what I told Father. I just feel a little bit funny about her right now."

She seemed to be asking a question that Mr. Pop did not want to answer. His eyes filled with tears.

"I just wanted to make her jump. I thought she'd like it if she gave it a try."

"I know." He turned away to hide his crying.

"Should I go get the flashcards?" she asked, suddenly compliant.

"Lump was great," said Mr. Pop, discreetly wiping at his eyes. "Lump was great. A great horse."

Kiki turned on one socked foot. "Back in a minute," she said, and thumped up the stairs.

When Mr. Pop had arrived for last week's lesson, Lump had been grazing in the paddock. The whir and the whip and the columns up above. The mountain looming behind. He'd come early to spend some time with her, and he had not been able to keep himself from running toward the white wooden fence.

"Hello Lump," he said, leaning over the fence. He stood on the bottom rung, felt it hard through his worn-out boots. "Woo-woo," he said, "woo-woo." He held out an empty hand.

Lump. Elegant Lump. Colorful Lump. She raised her head from eating and stared at Mr. Pop. When she looked at him, every inch of her body—hazel and toffee and auburn and rust and white—quivered with desire. "I know," he said to her. "But I can't. It is nothing. There is nothing."

She turned and offered him her profile. Her one black eye blinked once. The air between them was charged. He beckoned to her. "Lump," he said, nearly out of breath, "Lump, here I am. It was me, once. I was the apple. I was the apple."

She raised one hoof and was about to set it down at a friendly angle when Father threw open the stable doors and emerged holding a saddle under one arm and the not-small Kiki under the other. The saddle was broken, its horn was split. Kiki, slung about by Father, drooped lifeless as sea grass, uprooted and beached, over his massive arm.

"Yes!" screamed Father, "Yes, yes, yes, yes, yes!" He tossed the saddle over the fence and looked as if he would do the same to Kiki, but she wrapped her arms, slick and black in bloating sleeves, around his waist. "Wait," she said, "I want to do it myself. Like a grown up."

He put her down, and she hoisted herself up and rolled over the top of the fence with some difficulty, teetering there, her soft stomach folding over the wood.

"Good thing you're early, Pop Man," yelled Father across the paddock. "You're about to witness a rite of passage. Lump's getting mounted today!"

But something wasn't right. Father's mood was extra-undignified, his comportment frenetic. He ran back and forth along the fence, on his tiptoes, his arms flapping behind him like a king crane wild and swollen with grief, but he was smiling. His teeth were showing.

"What about the lesson?" said Mr. Pop, waving his best pouch of pens.

"The lesson can wait!" said Father. With beastly ease, he vaulted over the white fence and ran toward Kiki, who was now standing in the center of the paddock, holding the broken horn of the saddle.

Lump was turning nervously against the fence, as far from the three of them as she could get. Mr. Pop got down from the fence. He turned his back on the scene. Her name tumbled around inside his heart. *Lump. Lump. Lump.* She thrust up through the top of his skull. He dug through his hair and felt, with his empty hand, the contour of her body softly outlined in his bone. *Lump. Lump. Lump. I was the apple. It was me, once.*

He refused to look. There was activity increasing in the paddock. Sounds of struggle and speed. "Go," screamed Father. "Kick, kick, kick. Grab her mane! Grab her mane!"

Thud went the hooves of Lump. Her sounds were uneven, she stopped and she started. She pulled up short. Mr. Pop felt her fear and confusion. He tried to swallow it whole.

Kiki whimpered. "I can't," she said to Father. "Lump won't jump. She hates me. Lump hates me."

"Dig in," said Father. "Be hard with her. Be hard."

A column traveled overhead. Mr. Pop watched it go. He heard nothing but the anxious thud of Lump's hooves.

The helicopter moved across the valley. It traveled up the mountainside to where the pale pig slept in her pen of rebar and string. There she slept in the shadow of the great jointed tube that kept swallowing and swallowing the waterfall. The tube would never get full, and neither would the pale pig, who held in the bowl of her eye all the fruit that had ever been and all the fruit that would ever be. Her favorite were the infant fruits, those little buds that had hardly burst—they would never have the chance to spoil. These she held in the center of her eye. These she summoned with her killer gravity. She was hungry for what was still suckling at the teat of the tree, and she had many friends who would oblige her, who would ravage their private orchards just to earn her favor. And though he'd known that there was nothing he could offer her, he had not been able to resist. Mr. Pop had carried himself up the mountainside like a package full of treats, to be refused. Through the columns, he had shuffled, like the dog of his people, to her deceptively simple pen. There he had witnessed the awful truth of her appetite. Yes, his situation had been made quite clear, but he had come back down the mountainside terrorized by hope.

The helicopter disappeared over the mountain. Mr. Pop became aware of a silence at his back. There was no activity. No sound at all.

Mr. Pop knew he would have to see. Still he waited.

Then Father came up behind him, breathing heavily. That he was wet, that he was wet and stank of tar—Mr. Pop wished to wait.

"Pop Man," said Father. "You need to take Kiki inside. She's torn up."

Mr. Pop allowed himself to be taken by the arm and turned by Father. Kiki lay filthy and blank on her back halfway under the fence. "I can't make it," she whispered. "I'm too big."

"Here we go," said Father, pulling her the rest of the way. He picked her up and set her on her feet. Her legs collapsed beneath her.

"Lump can't," she sobbed. "Lump can't stand. I can't stand either."

Lump must have jumped, she must have tried. She had cleared the paddock fence but landed wrong. She lay on her side, and the broken saddle had slipped down around her stomach and wedged up hard against her hind legs. Mr. Pop walked toward her.

"Pop Man," said Father. A queasy little laugh. "Don't look. It'll stick with you."

Lump's front leg had been rearranged. Like a stair, it broke and rose and broke and rose, as if someone had slid a wide-toothed saw back and forth across her bone. She stared at him with her one black eye. A fly landed there, and she did not blink it away. It skated around on the black and shimmering surface of her agony. "Lump," he said. "Lump."

Father shuffled up. His wetness and his tar. "The worst," he said. "Isn't it? My luck is the worst."

"You'll shoot her?" said Mr. Pop, turning to go.

"Yep," said Father. "Yep, yep, yep. What else?"

Mr. Pop left Father and Lump and took Kiki by the sleeve. He pulled her toward the red house. "Pop Man," she said, crying, "Guess what? Lump never liked you. She told me so. She told me just the sight of you makes her want to kill herself."

No, he should never have come back to the red house. He should have refused, at the moment of Lump's jump and of her breaking, to return. No more lessons, no more words. No more.

But now it was too late, for here was Kiki with the stack of cards. She hopped, like a much smaller child, down the stairs.

"I couldn't find them at first, but then I did. They were hidden under the new kittens," she said. "So they're wet."

The cards were wrinkled and brown with birth-blood. "There are new kittens?"

"Yeah, the others disappeared. Father says they got eaten out in nature cause they had no brains. These new ones are better. They can hold their tongues inside their mouths so they don't look so stupid all the time."

Mr. Pop clenched his pouch of pens. "Miss Lister wants us in the kitchen today."

"No study, no problem," said Kiki. "I don't like it in there anyway. It smells."

He shivered with something like feeling for Kiki. "I'm sorry," he said. "It must still be very hard for you."

Kiki laughed. "Oh, I don't care about that, I just like to look out the kitchen window better."

At the low round table, they went through the cards onto which Mr. Pop, before he'd known what he was up against, had neatly inked a carefully selected set of words and their translations: balloon, castle, flying, mystery, swim. But Kiki had not responded. She had never practiced. She could not remember a single verb. She'd got a hold of some nouns, but she could not pronounce them correctly.

"Who cares," she said. "This is stupid. Anyone I could talk to is dead anyway." She lowered her eyes. "Except for you, Pop Man," she said. "I do like you. Do you like me?"

"Yes," said Mr. Pop, staring out the window at the empty paddock. "I like you, Kiki. Would you prefer dictation?"

"Not really!" she exclaimed.

Then Kiki jumped up onto her chair. She pulled her large shirt up and flapped it around excitedly, showing her pure white stomach, the line of red now cracked and weeping.

She poked at the wound and showed him her wet fingertip. "I'm going to let them taste it. They're so hungry, they'll probably lick it right up."

"Miss Lister," called Mr. Pop. "Come quickly!"

"She can't come," said Kiki, her eyes fixed on Mr. Pop. "Her TV show's on."

"I don't understand," he said, stepping side to side. "Something must be done."

Kiki flipped her tangled mass of hair. She got down off the chair and crossed her bloating sleeves. "You're afraid," she said.

He stared at her. He tried to find his sympathy. She was a child, after all. She had lost so much. "I am," he said. "Miss Lister!" he screamed, his head aflame.

"What was your wife's name again?" asked Kiki.

He breathed deeply. "Varvara," he said.

"What was she like?"

The letters she did not read. The daybook she did not open. The hearth she tended for him long after she was stiff. The vests she oiled. Her cracked spectacles. Her ripped pillow. Her steady, always modest, appetite.

"She was kind," said Mr. Pop. "Very kind. And merciful. She was—"

"Varvara," said Kiki, skipping toward the door. "I'm going to name the kittens Varvara."

Mr. Pop went to the window. He propped himself up on the kitchen sink. The wind twisted through the paddock, stirring the dirt. A short time later, he saw Kiki running through the browning fields. She was headed toward the mountain.

Miss Lister appeared in the doorway. She held a bowl of shining, clean-shaven roots.

"What is it?" she said. "My show is on."

"The new kittens," he said. "They're not being fed properly."

"Oh that," said Miss Lister. "It's not our house, Mr. P. We just work here. Not our concern. There are all kinds, Mr. P. All kinds."

The view was closing itself down. He thought of his long walk home along the dry riverbed, which was all that was coming for him.

"Go on home, Mr. P," said Miss Lister. "Take some time for yourself. You really aren't needed here. I can't see why he ever asked you to come. It'll make no difference what you do— she is not her mother's daughter. No, I'm never sure what he's thinking, or if he ever is—thinking. Most of the time I don't even know where he is. I just go on. Now you go on too."

Then the wind picked up and the stable doors flew open. Something was moving around inside. He leaned forward over the sink. It was Lump. She staggered out of the stable, her broken leg dragging in the dirt. She could lift it only so high. Like a stair, it broke and rose, broke and rose. Her lips stayed up over her teeth and her tongue hung down small and dry.

"Lump wasn't shot?" he said.

Miss Lister set her bowl on the kitchen table. She came to the sink and took his hand and stroked it with a feather from her pocket. "No," she said. "I thought he told you. Kiki was allowed to keep the horse."

"Not shot," he said. "Alive."

"I admit it's strange. It's not nice. Life can go so rotten. But at least she can still walk, after a fashion."

Lump was hungry. She crept toward the hay. Once near, she collapsed heavily onto her side and nibbled at the bale and chewed the hay and chewed her tongue along with it, her small dry tongue that was covered in dirt, and she closed her one black eye.

"Better she had never been born," said Miss Lister. "That's probably what you're thinking."

"No," said Mr. Pop. "No." Her name tumbled around inside his heart: *Lump.* "I would never take back her birth."

High up on the mountaintop—a numinous foam. A white wave was forming. It gathered and grew. Like a cloud, it heaped, then curled, folding forward. Down it came, spreading itself over the treetops. Mr. Pop saw the pale pig riding, riding, riding. Her pen would be empty now. Her temple, abandoned. The great jointed tube would go on swallowing and swallowing the waterfall, taking everything for itself. There would be nothing living there.

He had tried to keep himself from hope, but it had pursued him. It had followed him all the way here, to the dry valley, to the big red house, where neither he nor hope belonged—and now it could not be denied that she was coming. Riding high the devouring wave, with her small black eyes trained on him, the pale pig hungered. He wondered, then, his hands fluttering over his throat, if perhaps the situation had been...adapted.

One was always saying goodbye. See you later. Down the hatch. "Yes," said Mr. Pop, removing his shirt, "One is always saying goodbye. To some one or some thing. There comes a time for everyone"—he seized Miss Lister's hand—"and then, there comes another. Yes, Miss Lister, even *I* was eaten once!"

Monument

I RODE A TRAIN INTO THE GREEN VALLEY. TWIN SISTERS sat on the red seats facing me. They shared one shawl and a bunch of grapes. Their hair was one black heart that framed their heads, which were touching inside of their special and violent privacy. Together they read through a stack of letters, and I watched.

"B, who was S?" said one.

"I don't know, B, are you sure we knew an S?" said the other.

"Yes, B, listen to this: S, *I've run your question across the grate and can only answer no. No, you can't come another time. No, we can't play anymore. Please stop returning like a fool.*"

"B, how mean."

"B, this is your handwriting."

"Oh B, I remember he had an S on his shoes."

"Scarf or ball, B?"

"Ball."

"Good riddance, then."

One twin wrote a note to the other on the back of an international envelope. Her sister read it and nodded sympathetically. They looked at me, smiling like two nurses.

I stared out the window at the green valley. It sped away and sped away. Sometimes the green would stop and it was as if a black horn had thrust through the earth, and the view would go dark and smooth, and I would try to slow it down—was it the head and the beak of a crow, was it a fall of hair or an iron spike, or a portion of my house, my ruined house—what was it? But the green would return, the leaf-green valley with its leaf-green mind, which could never be the home of my heart.

The twins took photographs of each other inside the shawl. Each flash made them glow like a pink and living crystal.

"B, you are so beautiful."

"B, you."

"Look B, it's like we're in the pink desert with our bowls of tea."

"B, I miss it there."

"Me too, B."

"I know B, plus Fourth Prince."

"Yes, Fourth Prince."

"We never got his picture."

One of the twins wore slippers. They were backless and sideless and red with a little hood where she could slip her toes inside. I watched her put them on and take them off with each swing of her leg and thought of a magician I'd seen as a child, who had hidden his head inside a giant hat and then slowly removed the hat to show that he no longer had a face and, who, faceless, had pretended to try to comfort all the children. *Hoo, Hoo, Hoo*, he said, in a voice that bubbled up from somewhere beneath his skin, so that each of us was forced to imagine a hidden mouth, a trapped mouth, smothered and useless.

I wanted to stand and take a walk down the aisle but was afraid of falling. The valley was becoming narrow, the green and the green and the black horn were closing in.

I was on the way to visit my cousin who was on display in a research hospital. When I thought of him, I pictured his body: the three deep bowls in his chest. It was in the middle bowl that his heart had first shown itself, fluttering weakly beneath the skin before it finally broke through. Since I'd come home from the army, I'd grown two bowls of my own, and now I put my hand over the third, which had just begun to form, and thought hopefully of a future in which I might get to see the workings of my own heart but not have to see the thing itself. To see the pump beneath my skin—if only that could be the sum of my unusual experience. Maybe I would not have to suffer as my cousin did. Maybe it would not surface.

The train car smelled of seafood and disinfectant, the black horn came and went and the green was all around, and the twins ate candied rose petals over a photo album.

"Remember this, B?"

"Yes, B."

"The hidden arena."

"Musical reeds."

"We got shushed, B."

"I know, B, but they secretly liked it."

"The fun doesn't have to stop, B."

"No, B, we won't let it."

"What did he call us, B?"

"Who?"

"Fourth Prince."

"Black and wild, B."

"Are we, B?"

They let the question hang between them and smiled at each other, seeming to open and close their eyes in coded sequence.

Their blinking had a sound: the fall and snap of a sheet in the hands of a capable orderly. I saw their privacy pass between them and it was firm as bone and colored black and I began to think that I was witness to the pearl of the black horn and the pearl was two female twins in a black-heart frame. But the green kept flashing. It was my mind. I could not stop watching it go.

Then the bare toe of the red-slippered twin brushed against my leg. Its little touch rescued me from the window and the valley's pushy green, and then she slipped her toes back inside the red hood and seemed not to notice that anything had happened at all. I wanted to talk to her. I thought I might. She had made contact.

The train stopped. The conductor announced a delay. The train relaxed, the air was fresh, I could see people stepping out onto the grass.

"B, some air?"

"Yes please, B."

I steeled myself for the shock of their separate heads. They held the shawl between them like a length of rope as they moved away down the aisle.

My chest itched as if some tiny industrious man were scooping away at my skin. I looked and looked and finally spotted the twins in the narrow green field between the train and the valley wall, which rose almost vertically toward its saw-toothed top. They had spread their shawl on the grass and were lying face to face, pulling each other's hair and laughing. I thought, B, B, B, they must be, again and again, without breath, and I wanted to hear for myself—this wild repetition meaning a closeness such as I had never known.

I walked the length of the train, bashfully, apologizing to anything. When I stepped onto the grass, my ankle folded and I fell sideways like a noodle. Someone laughed, someone else burped.

The twins didn't notice me as I approached, so deeply were they B, B, B in the sun. But when I arrived, when I was standing over them like a blind giant, they silently made room for me, patting the spot where I was to sit. I joined them but they went on as if I were not there. I stared at my hands. I felt that my pants had shrunk. I was about to roll away through the grass and switch seats on the train and never again intrude on anyone, anywhere.

A little girl began to donkey kick in front of us. She kicked and stared, kicked and stared, not at me, but at the twins. She had a simple face, flat and even, her tiny features crowded up around her nose. Her glasses were huge—her eyes too. She had the look of a wild goldfish caught between two rough fingers. Somewhere, her parents were enjoying some good, good quiet.

She kicked again and couldn't keep herself from staring at the twins. She stared long enough that they stopped their B, B, B, and turned toward her, and one of the twins made a gesture like come closer, come on. But the girl just stepped around in a little square of grass, spooked, and I could see that she was searching for the perfect thing to say, the thing that would secure her release. She shut her giant eyes and screamed, "We have a new Pope!" and each echo of her announcement bubbled around in the valley and returned and returned and with each return gained a tone that the little girl had not given it, an adult tone, indicating sarcasm or exhaustion. The earnestness of her pronouncement was lost. She took off kicking toward the train.

"B, like a pigeon in the smoke."

"Just like, B."

Now they thought of me. Red slipper squeezed my shoulder. She spoke to me directly.

"Isn't this all highly natural? It takes me back. This valley. Far back. It goes deep. Fable-deep."

"B, you're right. Your eyes are pink."

Red slipper set her leg over my leg. She seemed to be setting some conditions. Her face floated in pink shadow and was the face of a wise and festive baby.

"Tell me the fable of this valley. You."

She pointed at me. My third bowl thumped. I thought of myself as an old man made of salt, thudding across a colorless bridge to black. Returning from black. I searched the edges of the valley for the darkest horn and saw only the leaf-green fall, without seam or break. So this is my mind, I thought. I'll tell. Sure, I'll tell.

"Okay," I began, "let me see."

I struggled past my tongue. She pressed my leg with her leg and her twin looked away, as if my voice, presenting itself, were immodest.

"The fable of this valley," I said, "begins with women. Women who worked in a tea field."

"Where?"

"Here."

"Right here? There's not even a shadow of a field."

"No, about a mile down."

"Go on."

I thought, This is where one would mine one's memory. This is where one would pretend, where the fable would fill up with familiar friends, where the teller would drape a curtain over all known players to make new players. I could barely begin. While I hurtled down the narrow green, how could I begin? I was away, I had always been.

I stuck my hand into the ground and felt the fleshy snap of breaking root. To the deep. That's where. In the bowl of my head. Through the window of the train—green, green, green, and black. I still had dreams of life.

"Bear with me," I said. "The women worked every day. Tirelessly. They knew very few people who were not themselves.

They were known to each other so deeply that if they were tired one of them could nap on behalf of them all, and so their work went well and they were admired for their industriousness and rewarded with time off that they never took.

"Visitors came through the valley often. This was once the way to the capital before the capital sunk and was covered by water and stone and then forgotten and rebuilt somewhere else, and the most frequent visitors were men traveling alone, on their way to find an opportunity or a cure. For the most part, the women weren't moved by these visitors; they worked and drank tea and spoke to each other only of what had happened yesterday and of what would happen tomorrow."

"B, is this right?"

"It's his fable, B."

"We are women too, B, and we cover it all."

"We do, B. We confer constantly."

"Without limit."

"Without."

"Wildly!"

The slipper had slipped off. Bravely, I took it in my hand and tried to hook its hood over her toes but missed, and missed again. I pawed at her foot with that feminine tool. The twins exploded like stars underground. They laughed and laughed and hugged and rolled away and rolled back.

Red slipper gently pushed me to the ground, her hand filling my third bowl. "This feels insane," she said. "Uncanny."

She knelt at my side and felt my first and my second and then took her twin's hand and helped her feel them too.

"B, feel."

"I feel, B. Three depressions, this one not as deep."

They ringed and rubbed my bowls with their same-shaped fingers. I tried to hover above the grass, not to require, not to weep. I told the tiny man, Shovel faster, make it deep, so they can feel. Open was the green and closed it was too and flash-ing, flashing, past the black of the horn. There was memory, forcing up through the earth, and I rose with it, hard, black and determined.

"One day," I said, "a man came to the valley. This man was in search of a monument. He'd learned of this monument when, eavesdropping by the quay, he'd heard a sea captain say to a lit-tle boy: A line of seals scooted out of the sea, they would not stop, they left the shore and went over the hill to the leaf-green valley, and on and on they went, and I followed, on and on un-til they reached a remarkable monument, someone's impossible erection—a thick black horn sticking up from the earth, high as the sky and wider than your mother's house—and what do you think the seals did? They scooted around the Black Horn, they circled it entirely, and then they went back toward the sea. But they were exhausted. They had dried out. All of them died in the sun of the valley, they rotted and sank into the ground. I'll tell you what, said the sea captain, lifting the little boy's shirt, Some journeys are not meant to be taken. Some journeys are deranged.

"And so, overcome by curiosity about the Black Horn, the man had come to the valley to see the monument for himself. When he asked the woman about it, he called it the Black Horn, as the sea captain had, but met with little success. Do you know about the Black Horn? he would ask a woman in the field, and she would float off between the tea plants and whisper to an-other woman and those two would link arms and move away to-gether, down the rows. This went on and on, resembling a formal dance with one desperate man in attendance. Finally, one of the women, before floating away, said, I've heard of it, but I've never seen it. No one here can help you. Go away."

My heart pounded in my third bowl. It was a skinned ani-mal that had come to dry out in the dip of my chest. The twins were sympathetic. "Slow down," they said. "We are listening. We are patient."

"He could not try forever," I said. "Not without reward. The man gave up. But he was upset. He'd traveled a long way to see the monument, but no one would help him."

"B, but why?"

"Trust the teller, B."

"No reason. He just wanted to see it," I said.

The train rumbled and shifted on its tracks.

I tried to sit up. They were not holding me down. Their hands were light, the air was light, the train was a big black sigh that had ended.

"So," I said, "the man set up camp near the field, but not too near, not wanting to alarm the women. He dealt with his disappointment by lying on his back in the leaf-green grass and threading the stars together."

"How lovely, B. He made a net."

"No, B. A scarf!"

"Yes, B, yes, B. I see it. I see it."

"Whatever you like," I said. "Whatever you like. So, as the man lay weaving a scarf from the sky, one of the women approached. It was the one who had earlier admitted having heard of the monument. She came with her hands over her mouth. She waited until she was sure he understood that he must stay quiet, and then she told him what she knew. Nobody speaks of the monument, she said, because one of us killed herself there. And why did she? the man asked."

The train sounded, the blast filled the valley. My heart quivered at the bottom of the bowl and blackness split my eye. Here was green across from green, I knew the color well, but blackness, oh blackness—I knew it better. I'd stood at its base, I could feel it, the rough, shingled skin of the horn of the earth, and my home was there, my ruin, in the shadow of the highest black. There was something I'd forgotten. It returned now, as the twins plunged their fingers toward my heart, as they slid down the side of my third and final bowl.

"Go on. Don't stop now."

"Make it sound. Make it move."

"B, do you feel it?"

"Yes I feel it, B."

The little girl, the pope's herald, appeared in a train car window. She stared at me as the train rocked forward and backward and as the horn sounded and sounded again. The twins took turns listening to my chest. Red slipper raised my shirt.

The little girl raised her shirt, too, and pressed her bareness against the window. She breathed against the glass, clouding her face so only her smoothness showed. It put me in mind of other shows, other feminine demonstrations, which were guileless and easy, but which split the green of the home anyway. The little girl disappeared from the window and was replaced by her mother, whose face floated before her large, shadowy body. She stared at me as if I'd crossed the awful distance.

Gently, the twins touched. They explored my skin and the spot barely covering my heart. At times, it seemed as if they were gently digging, gently as their curiosity would allow, and I thought, Fine, lay it bare, lay it bare.

"B, can it be?"

"Yes, B, we might get to see it."

"He made a scarf from the sky, B."

"Isn't this wild, B?"

I stood at the base of the Black Horn. A young woman stood there too, she smelled of grass. My ruined house smoldered in the shadows. The woman went gray before my eyes. *Are you dying?* I asked her. *I'm waiting for my man to show,* she said. And I thought to myself, I have been away too long. My home is black, my heart is black, my heart must rise through the valley's green. I must surface.

The train blasted and moved down the tracks. I sat up in the green and watched the black go away and the twins waved to me from the window as if they were just arriving in the heart of my home, as if they were back from a long, long trip, as if they loved me, and like a murderer who has forgotten his crime but has long suspected the blackness of his heart, I turned away from all women and waited for the thing to show.

The Refugee

BRIAN ED WAITED OUTSIDE OF THE RATION HOUSE on his long feet. Merlijn took his time coming to the door and opened it slowly. Brian Ed raised his hand and waved, and Merlijn smiled an embarrassed smile and held up four fingers.

"No rations until four o'clock, Brian Ed."

"Yes," said Brian Ed. He stayed. He didn't leave. "How are you today?"

"Oh," said Merlijn, his hand on the doorknob. "I'm well, Brian Ed. Thank you for asking."

They stood in silence. Brian Ed shrugged. All courtesies escaped him. His everyday pack squeezed his neck and tore at his shoulders. Inside were the children's book, the cowgirl brooch, the old orange balloon— now deflated—that had once read *Welcome Refugee!*, and four heavy stones he carried without knowing why, each of these the size of a baby's head.

"Well," said Merlijn, patting Brian Ed on the hand. "See you at four, then."

Brian Ed thrust his long foot forward. "No," said Brian Ed. He thought of the book. "How is the weather? No snow will come? No avalanche?"

Merlijn smiled. He stepped out of the house and closed the door behind him. "Brian Ed," he said, "Are you hungry? Can I offer you a peach?" He cupped his hand as if the peach were there already, holding it up to Brian Ed's mouth. "Summer is coming. Sun. The peaches are good. No avalanche. Let's walk."

Brian Ed wasn't hungry. What he wanted was not material, but it was his own fault if Merlijn thought so. He only ever came to Merlijn for his ration—food, clothing, wood. Never had he come for company, not to Merlijn, nor to anyone else, not since the poison dropped and travel home became impossible. He'd never dreamed it would last three years, three was as long as some lives, he hadn't prepared and he hadn't adjusted. He hadn't learned the words. Instead, he'd gone dull in the comfortable glow of the golden cone.

Brian Ed followed Merlijn up the hill to the orchard, where peaches and cherries and pears hung huge from their trees, pulsing and oozing like the separate chambers of one metastasizing heart. This wild growth was one of the uglier effects, and Brian Ed could barely look.

Merlijn picked a peach and the sound of it detaching from the branch, the deep suck and slip, turned Brian Ed's stomach. "Here you go," said Merlijn. "Nobody's gotten sick yet."

Brian Ed took a bite and the flesh of the peach squirmed against his teeth, as if it were a living thing that did not intend to go down easy.

Merlijn watched him eat. He wiped juice from the sides of Brian Ed's mouth with the back of his hand. Brian Ed pulled a string of pulp out of his throat. It was thick and solid as a rat's tail.

"Merlijn," said Brian Ed. "Merlijn." He dropped the peach and tried to say things with his eyes. When that failed, he said, "I'm not hungry. What do you like to do? What are your favorites?"

The birds were growing back, and their calls were sharp and elated. The two men looked around the orchard, but the sound was coming from somewhere else.

"Funny," said Merlijn, "I thought flight was gone forever. But life finds a way, doesn't it." He narrowed his eyes.

"Brian Ed," he said, "Are you sure you're getting enough to eat? How is the hut? Summer is coming, did you get your tar? Are you sleeping? You know that you have our sympathy, you can ask us for anything. What do you need? Tell me what it is. I'll submit the request. I'll write it down for you. What is it?"

Brian Ed skirted the edge of the golden cone, he tried not to slip down the fade, though it was golden there and quiet and full of sense. Stay here, he begged himself, This is it. You are cut off. This world is the world. This end is the earth.

"Merlijn," he said, "I am trying to ask you: What do you like to do? For fun?"

"Brian Ed!" said Merlijn, his eyes suddenly awake. He slapped the trunk of a tree and six fleshly pears made dents in the earth where they fell. "You owl in the moss!" he exclaimed. "We never thought you would. You're learning! You're learning! How? Who's teaching you?"

"The book," said Brian Ed. "The book is teaching me!" He was moved to embrace Merlijn. They held each other and swayed back and forth. The shape of Merlijn, the fat square of his body, his warmth, the slim cushion on his back. Brian Ed shivered. Life could be just the same.

"This is wonderful," said Merlijn, holding him close. "Which book?"

Brian Ed said nothing. He looked down at the sea that had grown a hundred hands and he watched them slap at the young birds and suck them down to drown. He took off his pack and handed the children's book to Merlijn.

"*The Witch and the Avalanche*," said Merlijn. "I haven't seen a copy of this in a long time. Where did you find it?"

Brian Ed touched the word: *Where. Where.* Much of these three years had been a searching crawl, he'd been low and found things there, some devastating, some useful. Had he found this word? He had. But where had he been?

"Where," said Merlijn sternly, "did you find this book?" He pointed his finger and swung it around his head, drawing the limits of their world.

Brian Ed had found the book almost three years ago behind the abandoned kindergarten, back when he was still wiping himself with trash and nursing his burn and sleeping behind the well full of dead cats. Before the town had given him the hut.

"Where are the kids," said Brian Ed faintly. "There is the book, where are the kids."

Merlijn hugged himself, then touched the top of his nose. He turned away as if to examine a secret wound. Quietly, he echoed, "Where are the kids."

Where. Are. Where. Are. "No," said Brian Ed. He saw his company slipping away. He stretched like an athlete and shook free of his dullness. "No," he said triumphantly. "Where the kids *were*. Where they *were*. With books."

"Oh," Merlijn said, returning to the conversation dampened. "The kindergarten? I thought all of that went to the museum. But you got a piece of it. You got a little piece of it." He rubbed the sides of his face. "I guess that's fine. You need it."

Merlijn ran his hand over the cover of the book. On it, a baby dangled from the highest branch of a tree. The baby hung there by its bonnet strings, above a town just destroyed by an avalanche. All was snow except for the pink baby in its tree, the brown tip of the church steeple poking through, and the very top of the red-hot staff of the witch that would soon melt her free. Merlijn's face turned a color that gave it texture and depth, dotted red, dotted white, dotted pink.

"When I was young," said Merlijn, "my sympathies were with the witch. She was desperate. To a child, desperation is poignant. I didn't know desperation then, not really. I thought I did. I knew I wanted things that I couldn't get. But real desperation, the kind that sends you down the tube—I had no idea. I read this book to Ingrid. Twice, maybe, before. You won't understand all of this, but I have to say it."

Merlijn bent at the waist and choked. A string of drool dangled from his mouth. Brian Ed touched Merlijn's back, he pushed his fingers in gently and felt the sweetness of the man's give. "I'm sorry," said Merlijn. "This is why I've never been to the museum."

"Okay," said Brian Ed. "Okay, okay." The body, he understood. The fold. It was the horror of dangling safely above the disaster, the same disaster that had folded him.

"I also, Merlijn, I also," said Brian Ed. He felt giddy with this sharing, it had been so long.

"You too?" said Merlijn, looking past Brian Ed. "Yes, of course. Anyone you once knew is good as dead."

"Yes," said Brian Ed, not quite catching on. He looked where Merlijn was looking, up the hillside at his hut that winked at them with its saggy eyes. The golden cone had settled there. He couldn't go back, not for a while, though the effort of conversation was great.

"What have you been doing up there all these years?" asked Merlijn with a sudden coldness. "What did you get up to— up there—all alone in your hut? That's a long time without anyone, without needing anyone. Did you have a friend? Any friend? A pet? What did you have? What did you do?"

Brian Ed didn't understand. He nodded. He put his pack on and felt the four stones grind against the small of his back. "Eat with me," said Brian Ed. "At night."

Merlijn smiled and shook his head no. He started back toward the ration house, and Brian Ed followed. "Thank you, Brian Ed," he said." I like what you're trying to do—this reaching out. But I can't tonight. There's a wedding in the village. Tord and Aud, the hang-gliders. You don't know them, do you? Of course you don't. You will, though. Now you will."

Brian Ed nodded and smiled. "Eat with me."

Merlijn said nothing.

"At night," he said again.

In the hut, it would be the same. He would feed himself barely enough and then lie in ruins on the six planks that were his bed, thinking about color and shape, sliding along the edge of the fade.

It would go: Circle is blue or black. The hour of cold. The ocean's eye. Triangle, the purple swimmer, intersects the afternoon. Square all orange, some red, in the morning. Rise with sister. Sister is cone, golden cone, she must be circled to be seen. Circle is blue or black—backward through the day. And so on to the far side of night, nothing gained, nothing learned. Nothing new.

"No dinner," said Merlijn. He stood in front of the ration house door. "No. Dinner. Would you like your ration now?"

"No," said Brian Ed. He curled his dry hand into the other. He would not leave.

Merlijn looked him up and down, as if he were seeing Brian Ed for the first time. The midday work horn sounded. Neither of them moved. The horn sounded again, and Merlijn sighed. "Of course," he said. "You'll come to the wedding."

Brian Ed shook his head. "Come. Come?" He wasn't sure.

"Not as a guest," said Merlijn. "Not that way. There's a tradition in this village, a fun one. If you live in the village but aren't invited to a wedding, you are allowed to come after midnight, but only in disguise. It's called playing ghost. That's all you'll have to do—find a costume. But then you can eat and drink and join in. Why not, Brian Ed? Why not?"

Merlijn vanished inside the ration house. Brian Ed waited, though he wasn't sure for what. He still hoped, dimly, for a dinner companion. But when Merlijn emerged from the dark doorway, he was holding a pair of pointed boots, a full-moon mask made of white feathers, and a woman's cape.

"These," said Merlijn. "You'll wear these."

He shoved the costume toward Brian Ed, who backed away. Merlijn held up ten fingers, then two. Ten, then two. "Midnight," he said. "Put these on and go to the wedding at midnight. For fun. Fun, Brian Ed. Remember fun?"

Merlijn was gritting his teeth. The cape fell out of his hands onto the ground, and he made no move to pick it up. Brian Ed bent down to get it and saw that Merlijn's left shoe no longer had a sole. Quickly. Quickly, or the cone. He took the mask and slipped it over his head and the feathers stuck to his lips.

"Just like that," said Merlijn, "you are the moon." He rolled his neck around and shook his legs as if he'd just been released from a long confinement. "At midnight, go to the folk house."

Brian Ed shook his head. It might come gold. What sister said, the same old. If he didn't try. "The folk house," he said. "I don't know."

"Okay, let's see," said Merlijn. "Near the memorial."

"Memorial," said Brian Ed.

"For the dead."

"No."

"The memorial that disappeared."

"No."

"The four stones."

"Stones?"

"Yes. Where the four stones were. Where they used to be."

"Oh," said Brian Ed. "The four."

"Yes, there. The building next to the place where the four stones were. With the grass roof." Merlijn knelt and ripped some grass out and threw it on the roof of the ration house. "In the garden behind the folk house. Get it?"

Brian Ed nodded. "See you," he said.

"But I won't see *you*," said Merlijn. He winked at Brian Ed and his lashes became spider legs and kicked and kicked and kicked.

AT MIDNIGHT, BRIAN ED—IN POINTED BOOTS, FULL-MOON mask, and woman's cape—approached the folk house. His face itched, but he would not scratch it, afraid to reveal himself. His long feet suffered in strange boots, the woman's cape slipped off his shoulders and dragged behind him like a train.

The wedding party was in full swing. Three large women stood on tree stumps and performed a traditional dance. A man with a limp mustache bit quickly and furtively into a large leg of meat. The garden was lit by four small fire pits, their smoke moving straight up in polite, restrained columns. There were others in costume, fewer than ten, only one of them appeared to be a woman. She wore a robe made of coarse tassels that rearranged themselves as she moved so that the shape of her body was obscured and her mask was the face of a brown bear. A tiny cat moved through the party unnoticed, eating food that fell to the ground.

Brian Ed moved into the crowd. He spotted Merlijn, who was drinking from a pink fluted glass, laughing and swinging his arms. Brian Ed waved, and Merlijn stared at him as if he were a stranger and went on laughing and swinging, then emptied his glass and moved deep into the crowd where Brian Ed could not see.

There were no chairs at the party. Brian Ed stood near this table and that, blushing beneath his mask. Stay, he begged himself, This is it. This is what is.

The bear-faced woman floated by. As she passed, she whispered, "I know you. The refugee. But you aren't that. You're a tourist, and your trip won't end."

End. End? He could not arrive at its meaning. He watched the woman spin herself around. She reached up, pinched the air and drew it down, pinched the air and drew it down, until she was covered in night, and he could no longer tell where she was.

He drifted along the outskirts of the party, listening to conversation, listening to words. Some he knew and some he didn't, and there was pleasure in guessing. He began to enjoy himself. He thought, My back and neck are free tonight. I am here, and I am not here. A thought of his hut arrived, and it was, for the first time, a happy one. I will be there alone, but I will not be sick with myself. He grabbed a bun and bit into it. Cream burst into his mouth, and his knees trembled. He wanted to sit but there were no chairs at the party.

A drunk man grabbed Brian Ed and drew him to his side. He was speaking to a group of six. None of them were in disguise. Brian Ed took them in. They had the town's complexion, pale and even, the gray-blue eye all around.

"As I was saying," said the man, "we had no idea what we were up against. We let war sneak up on us like a man playing ghost at a wedding." He winked at Brian Ed.

The six pale faces murmured their agreement.

"Yes, oh yes, oh yes."

"It snuck up. It did."

"And the reason we didn't see it coming," he went on, "is very simple—*we* are simple. We think our enemy is unknowable.

We are good and our enemy is evil. We extend no sympathy to him, he is a stranger, and we are wary of strangers. And we prefer to think this way because the truth is much more devastating. The truth is complicated. Not so! you say. We are simple people! We live simple lives in the snow! We do not deal in the intricate. Our summers are the shortest in the world! Our truth is simple! Well, I say it's not!"

He squeezed Brian Ed. "Do you know the truth?" he asked Brian Ed, blowing warm ripe air into the eyeholes of his mask. Brian Ed closed his eyes against the waving feathers. He shook his head no, though he was not sure what had been said.

"No," said the man. "No, you don't. Someone get me another drink." He wiped his face on his wide yellowed collar. He stomped his foot on the ground and spooked the tiny cat, who ran around in circles holding an olive in her mouth.

The man waited with his hand outstretched until someone filled it with drink. He licked something green from the rim of the glass and took a sip.

"The truth is," he said, pausing for effect. "The truth, the real truth, is this—war is right foot versus left. What do you think of that?" His eyes popped and he leaned toward the six pale faces. The faces smiled politely and waited an appropriate length of time before turning away like six planets spinning the way they must.

The man slumped against Brian Ed, who held him and patted his back in a brotherly way. "It's awful now," said the man. "Everything is awful."

"No, no," said Brian Ed, "okay, okay." And the man straightened up and peered into the mask and suddenly needed no support. "I see," said the man. "You finally decided to join us. You finally came down from your hut."

The party was changing. It got loose and turned its face. More ghosts arrived in costume. Someone played a small drum and everyone looked up at the dark sky. "Oooh," they said, as a shape floated down. It came beautiful and slow like a giant rainbowed moth. It was Tord and Aud, the newly married, gliding to earth on their vast shared wing.

Brian Ed bowed his head. The feeling was gold and warm and familiar. It could not be shared. The shape grew up around him and inside was the same, was sister. He was at home. Please, she said, war is real, and he said, How can it be? I've never seen it, and she said, Don't go, Brian Ed, not now, and he said, I will go. Your fear is your fear.

To the hut, to the hut. He must get back, he must get in. But Merlijn approached. He was holding the hand of a young woman in green and his teeth were stained gray. "Merlijn," said Brian Ed, reaching for his face and Merlijn frowned and dodged his reaching hand and said, "Tsst, that's not how it goes." He led the young woman away, though she kept spinning around on her toes to stare at Brian Ed. "Is it him?" she said loudly. "Is it really?"

Two fiddlers began to play. The song surprised. It was atonal, it jerked alive and fainted away. As if on cue, the ghosts all gathered in the center of the party, and Brian Ed tried to leave, he tried to sneak away, but he was hemmed in by a fence of arms and herded toward the center.

The ghosts stood close and their heavy costumes made it warmer than night. There was some purposeful shifting, and Brian Ed let himself be moved and moved until he was standing in the center of the group with the bear-faced woman. Her expression was the bear's expression. It was unreadable. She touched his feathered face.

The music stopped. The ghosts opened up and formed an aisle. Merlijn waited at the end, holding the little cat. The music began again and it was ponderous and heavy and dark. The bear-faced woman took his arm. "Now we march," she whispered. "Follow me, tourist."

They moved together down the aisle. Brian Ed nodded to the masks as he passed. The weight of the woman's arm was welcome. He smiled beneath his feathers, undetected in his happiness. Merlijn was smiling too and stroking the little cat. Brian Ed pulled the woman closer to him, and she came. It's not so bad. It could be the same. Life, the world, this trip.

They arrived at the end of the aisle, and Merlijn began to speak in a deep and meaningful voice. "Lovers," he said. "We are witness to your love. We love your love. Do you promise to tend it? Will you take care?"

Brian Ed leaned in. He tried to whisper to Merlijn, who would not come close. "Love," he said. "Love?"

"Yes," hissed Merlijn. "Just say yes." Loudly, he said again, "Will you take care?"

"Yes," said the bear-faced woman.

"Yes," said Brian Ed.

"Lovely," said Merlijn. "Whereas before you were like two strangers gulping from a cloudy mug, now you share one clean glass. Ghosts, you are married. Ghosts, you are joined forever."

The crowd cheered, and Brian Ed spun around. *Married. Married?* He turned the word over in his mind. Is it so easy? Is life? He stared at the bear who was his wife and felt the coarse tassels of her fur. She came closer. "That was fun, right?" she whispered to him, and he said, "Fun, fun. Yes, it is fun."

It is so easy, fun. Fun is easy. He was filled with a feeling he'd thought was long gone, and the feeling was serious. He twirled his wife around and grabbed her around the waist. She laughed high and happy. "I love," he said, "I love."

But when he went to raise her mask, to reveal her face, to kiss the woman and not the bear, she screamed and slapped him hard and feathers floated from his face and his eyeholes rearranged. In the dark of his mask, he made a sound that disappeared.

"Brian Ed," he heard Merlijn say. "Brian Ed, I'm sorry. That was just part of it. Part of playing ghost. There is always a fake marriage to shadow the other. Fake. Fake. Not real. Do you understand? Fake."

Brian Ed adjusted his mask so that he could see. The other ghosts had removed their masks and their paleness overwhelmed. He looked at the ground. The little cat was choking. He walked toward it, wanting to help, but the crowd gasped and blocked him with their bodies.

"No," they said, "Don't let him get the cat! Don't let him touch the cat! It's the refugee! The refugee! He's after the cat! Don't let him near the cat! Don't let him near the cat!"

The Colonel

THE FRINGE-FOOTED PONY DANCERS WERE performing in the courtyard.

"Sometime last night," said Goro, "the dancers were let loose."

"Who did it?" I asked.

"You," he said.

Goro held his snips aloft.

"Snip," said the man whose hair he was cutting.

"Snip," went Goro.

"What about," I suggested, "lending me those snips?"

I smiled in the doorway. I blocked his shop.

"What about letting me," I said, "snip a little something?"

Goro sheathed his snips in a white leather pouch. He knew me too well. In fact, he knew it all.

"No way," said Goro. "I like the dancers' moves. That fringe is hot stuff, to me."

"Uh oh," said the man in the chair. "At this point, I'd like to assert my total blankness. My opinions moved away, many years ago. I've lived without—quite comfortably! Don't try to get *me* involved."

Goro unsheathed his snips and cut away the man's shirt collar. He slung the collar over his shoulder and blew on the man's neck. Then he spit on it and rubbed the spit in. The man groaned.

"Settle down, guy," said Goro. "The Colonel and I have an understanding. I wrote the poem for his newborn."

Goro snipped away. He didn't flinch and neither did the man whose neck he was kissing with his razored beak. By Goro, I was made quiet. Always and finally by Goro, by his tools and his snips and his pen that wrote her poem, which he let peek over the top of his shirt pocket to remind me.

I hadn't been after a bad day, but a bad day had begun without me. I looked from Goro to the courtyard. My pike was where I'd left it, leaning against the shuttered window of the toy shop. The gourd was beginning to smell. Four months I'd had it, and just now it was turning from green to black. Soon the pike would bust through its top, and the gourd would slide down fast or slow, smearing itself all over my only tool of ruling.

Outside was a scene—hot, but not the kind Goro liked. Turmoil. Dust. Fringe. Metallic tightness. Women flung about in wanton horsie dance. The brittle sound of the cackle-horns over the half-drowned bong of the church bell. Men with cabled arms. The catchings. Practiced whacks. The yawning feminine crevasse crammed full of laboratory muscle. And the thud-thud hoof, the cultured, keratinised foot, bred toeless through the years, that would never, no matter how close it got, be the thing it was aiming to be.

"If I am to be the Colonel," I said. "If I am—"

"Self-appointed," said Goro. "Colonel says you."

"All the same."

Snip. "Not at all the same."

"The preferment was passed up by everyone but me."

"Because nobody wanted it. A colonel, the idea of a colonel, is dead," said Goro. He bent to tuck his pants tighter into his fancy boots. The pen in his pocket threatened to slip. Behind him on the wall of his shop were three photographs. A beehive, ten crows on a high-flying line, and the impression of a paw in purple mud.

"Not everyone thinks so," I said. I looked for affirmation to the man in the chair, who was newly shorn and silent. "Don't you long for deep affinities?" I asked him. "Don't you hate to be reminded—imperfectly?"

The man sucked on his lip. He opened one side of his mouth as if he were about to speak, then slipped a cube of yellow cheese inside. His jaw rearranged as he chewed, his face two halves of a square that ground together.

"They're popular, those dancers," said Goro. "Look at the crowd they draw. You like them too, don't you, Noll? Don't you dream of the dazzle and flip?"

"Colonel," I insisted.

Goro rolled his eyes. "Yes, Noll. That's what I said. Colonel. Noll, there's another side of things. There's the pleasure side. Two bunks—top and bottom. Different atmospheres. You're stuck on that bottom bunk. Where's your crowd? Have you noticed? You don't have one."

I couldn't deny that the crowd outside was big. Young adults and old adults and very old adults. Some removed their flat-topped hats. Some, out of habit, dragged their empty red wagons behind. Stationless, they stood in the shade of the purple awning sipping from hairy bowls through long glass straws. No one seemed to have come with anyone else. There were no pairs or groups or intimates. The adults circulated endlessly, sipping from this straw or that, pausing to talk to anyone they met.

The pony-dancers stomped. The cackle-horns sped up. Unnatural fringe. Applause. The red dirt floor was raised. The dancers and their audience hovered above the earth.

"It's not right," I said.

"Nobody cares what you think," said Goro.

It was warm outside. The oily gourd was getting stronger, meatier. I turned around in the doorway and thought of sitting down in the shop for a cut. Goro tapped his fancy boots, which were cloaked in his customer's wispy hair. The hair sifted down to the floor and disappeared into the rosy tile.

"All the same," I said, enfeebled. "If I am to be the Colonel—"

"Let us have our ponies," said Goro. He was angry. "We can't have them real. None of us will ride again. No speed, no mane in the wind of speed. No speed! Let us have whatever ponies we can get!"

He spun the man in the chair and stacked his head on top of his customer's so that they were a four-eyed totem. "Let us," he said, gesturing to their heads, "have what we want."

The man in the chair let his lips droop down. *Sorry*, he mouthed.

"We'll never think of them as ponies," I said to the man in the chair, encouraged. "You and me, we'll never make that mistake. A true hoof, a hoof absolute, has no fringe! It is attached to a horse!"

I went to shake the man's hand, but Goro brandished his snips. "Out," he commanded. "Enough of you today."

I left the doorway. The doorway was free. They were free— of me. And I was free too, and everyone in the courtyard was free, over-free, and dancing or watching the dance or watching the fringe fly around or dreaming a deranged hoof-dream, a dream that got it slightly wrong.

I and my pike and my skewered gourd circumambulated the crowd. The red dust hung in the air. The glass straws ended in hairy bowls, switched bowls indiscriminately, tinging delicately against the sides of things. Adults sipped in the violet shade. The grocer moved through with his heavy tray. "Fried pellets," he warbled. "Fried pellets for sale. Enlivening. Rejuvenating. Fresh use. Salvaged bits. Bite the bits."

To be sure, the bad day had begun without me. The dancers had not slept. All night they'd scraped the closet door with their performance accessories, with their silver stars and glitzy blinders. But I'd held fast, I'd thrown the cushion from the wooden chair. When they tired of scraping, they talked to me through the door, nonsense talk, performative and overly gay: "Colonel, let us flip for you." "Sandra will do the special V." "Won't you, Sandra, the unthinkable V." "Not pony-possible, but that's the perk of pretending." "Come on, Noll—"

"Colonel," I asserted.

"Come on, Colonel. We know the door isn't locked."

They laughed brightly. They teased. But I had a book, and I read the book, and sure I was frequented throughout the night by the V, by the thought of the V, but my strength was greater than any unthinkable pose, my strength was rooted firmly in the possible, the pony-possible. I deferred to the limits of the old world. My pike was near, my gourd was rightly poked, I had my book and my book was fine. There was a whale in the book, but not a dream or a shade—a real blubber body, a whole animal returned, containing in its interior a wet layer of mystery, a submerged revelation, something to slosh through in search of—in spite of?—my mind.

At some point in that flu-long night, I must have fallen asleep—the hours spun. I dreamt myself onto the tongue of the whale and was on my way down, feet up in the air, head pressed into the pink, delighted to see that the table, in the whale's belly, was formally set and covered in damask, and that my name hung from the back of a chair, and next to it hung no other name and no other name and no other name, all down the line, when a sudden quiet intruded on my rest, and I woke to find the closet door wide open and the dancers gone.

The dancers had escaped to perform another day, and so they did. I held my pike that meant nothing and worried on the edge of the crowd. The purple awning wouldn't allow our height, mine and my pike's, and the gourd, heating, accelerated toward rot. It grew black as my mood. No one greeted me; the adults sidled away.

On the crowd, correspondence was lost. A green gourd on a pike, a simple, living ball—a natural ball—did not resonate. Embodiments, no. Mysteries, no. They preferred the ponied foot, the dream, the shade, the doctored resurrection (it would rot, too, and faster). This was not the way to recover the world.

The dance came to an end. The dancers, breathing, bowed. It was my turn. Holding the pike straight, I made my way to the panting center, where all the dancers hugged and kicked and stretched, and, though they made way for me, though they enveloped me (took me right up), laughing, slapping me on the back, saying "Good morning, Colonel, good morning," as if the night before had made us friends and I their friendly ruler, the adults were not happy. The men and the women booed. I was booed. The Colonel.

"Gooey staff," someone yelled. "Close your closet," said someone else.

Pellets were thrown. They landed at my feet and broke apart and inside were little teeth. A dying caterpillar, red and yellow and crowned, moved slowly across a dancer's unsound footprint and mounted one of the teeth and curled itself around the tooth as if it were still alive and capable of guarding a prize. My feet went dead. I clung to my pike for support.

"Stick in the mud," said someone. "Nobody," said someone else.

Goro appeared in the doorway of his shop. He flashed his snips about, he flashed his fancy boots. He held his pen in his hand and wrote letters in the air as if by cruelty he could stop me. I showed my gourd to him. Deep in my gourd was a soul, the soul of the natural world, which was greater than his snips, and I was a plainer man, a more possible man, and my dreams were more possible too.

"Noll, go home," he said. "Go home."

A dancer in metallic tightness, a woman, wrapped her hand around my hand that held my pike. Her fringe was long and dirty and red. She was warm from the dance. "Colonel," she purred.

I looked at her. Damp hair framed her face, which was awake but sleeping too. "Sandra," I said, shaking her off, rattling the gourd. "Don't touch me."

The dancers stepped back. They frowned. Their pleasantness disappeared. "Get him, Sandra," they said. "Show him."

The graveled blast of a cackle-horn sounded. Sandra backed away from me. "I feel so sorry for you and your gourd," she said. She got on her back in the red dirt and raised her legs above her head. Her fringe hung down and showed her half-formed hooves.

I covered my eyes. The crowd cheered.

"Impossible pose," they cooed.

"I'm showing you, Colonel," said Sandra. "I'm making the V."

"Unthinkable," yelled Goro, delighted.

I ran toward his voice.

"No you don't," Goro said. "No you don't!" and closed the door to his shop.

I burst upon the glass of his door with such force that the gourd came loose from my pike. But it did not slide down. The gourd tore off and hurtled through the air and smashed beneath the purple awning. A bird darted out from its dark insides, shaking itself free in the air, seeds plopping wet on the red ground.

The courtyard melted. Adults on their knees. Wagons rolled loose. The glass straws shattered as the hairy bowls were tossed. I stared at the gourd that had fed the bird for months, at the pulp that had been its secret nest, secret even from me, from the Colonel, and I felt the full weight of the mystery I'd nurtured without knowing why. This was the body of what we'd lost. Not a soul or a dream or a shade, but a wholeness returning, a portent, perhaps, of other homecomings.

The bird flew freely, naturally, in the light. Across the bright sun. Diving and looping, tracing some age-old pattern. Goro joined me in the courtyard. Together we looked up.

"I'm filled by this," Goro said. "I'm full. My hand moves toward my pen."

The crowd was alive to me: "Are you a magician?... Is this a performance?"

"No," I said. "I'm not even here."

The adults had gathered in the center of the courtyard. The dancers, too. There was fringe over fringe and Sandra making the V, and I did not even mind it, because everyone loved the bird that I had brought. I was their leader, after all, and this was where I had led. Naturally.

Briefly, the bird hung like a star above the crowd. It spiraled slowly down and paused and beat its wings once. Then it dove and dove and the crowd made way and it headed toward Sandra, Sandra in the V, the not-possible V, beyond which a darkness had gathered, darker than any closet I had ever known. The bird gained speed and dove toward the V, and I feared the bird's vanishing so much that I could not breathe. Down the bird went, streaking toward darkness. But I was the Colonel now, I was not Noll. I would not let it go.

I ran toward the V, my pike in hand. For the briefest of moments, I kept pace with the bird. We met in the air. I looked into its eye and saw a foreign field teeming with life, crowded with cradles, thundering with herds. There, I thought. There.

Then the bird shot ahead. It was intent on darkness, stupid thing. Down toward the V. It would vanish. It would go. "Here birdie birdie birdie," I pleaded. "Here. Stay here."

But the bird didn't stop. Its beak would enter. Next, its head. And then it would be gone. But I was the Colonel now, I would not let it go. Before the darkness could take it, I thrust my pike at the bird. Easily, the pike entered the body. It left a neat hole and kept on going. I could see the body beating. The pike went on and on. Through the hole it had made in the bird. Through the bird and past the bird. The V snapped shut. The bird, though it struggled, struggled in my sight.

"Noll, no!" screamed Goro.

The crowd came to get me, but I didn't care. The world would not leave me again.

Armand

Tʜᴇ ʀᴇsᴇᴀʀᴄʜ ʜᴏsᴘɪᴛᴀʟ sᴇɴᴛ ᴛʜʀᴇᴇ ᴅʀɪᴠᴇʀs—
one for each day of travel, one for each highway. He was
the last. Armand.

I didn't ask the name of the first, a twilight fellow in gray,
nor did he offer, but when he pulled into my driveway, emerged
from the car, and turned to the snow, I could see that he was
terrified. It must have been his first time.

He took my single bag. His hands were shaking. "Brr," he
said. Then, boldly: "Are you the brother?"

"The father," I said.

"Your daughter?" he asked.

"My son."

We traveled the rest of the black highway in silence. He
drove the hairpins slowly so that I did not feel ill. I watched the
road drop down into the forest and saw the snow-fed streams
(water, liberated) for the first time in my life and felt only a minor, yellowed awe. Near dawn we skirted the rim of the canyon,

and the highway turned from black to red. I folded and folded the note that was permitting my travel until it was hard and small.

The first trade-off took place at a checkpoint near a crumbling dam. Great bursts of water. Great rumblings. The first driver waved goodbye, closed the pedestrian gate behind him, and drifted away down the mesquite aisle. The second, Boris, sank into the driver's seat and asked if I wanted to take a picture.

"Of what?" I asked.

"Of the breaking. It's historic."

"No," I said. "The dam doesn't interest me."

That was the extent of our conversation. We followed the red highway through a leaf-green valley. We passed a black horn jutting up through the earth without saying a word, or stopping to see, or reflecting. The rest of the way was turquoise salt fields and hide-homes tearing in the hot wind.

We, each of us, pretended to be alone. My thoughts were not on the waiting body, on Ophi's body, as they should have been. My thoughts were not on the middle-of-the-night lapses, the times when I left him alone with his deepening bowl, to cry, to cry out for me. The unthinkable time when I lost my cool. The time of the too-rough bath. My thoughts were on some woman I'd met thirty years ago outside of the fish market and known for just a single night.

The final trade-off took place while I was asleep. When I woke up, Armand was already there in front of me, as if he had always been, his thin brown hair electrified, his beautiful hands on the dark wheel, his massive shoulders hanging before me, the highway no longer red, but white. The note permitting my travel was not in my hand. I searched the floor of the car. I lifted my feet. Nothing.

"Quickly," Armand said, pointing to a spot in the road.

An armored animal I had never seen, the back of it crushed, was dragging itself toward the side of the road.

"Poor thing," I said. "What is it? What is it called? What would you call it?"

"No, not there," said Armand. "There. Look there."

He pressed on the brake and glanced in the rearview mirror to make sure there was no one coming up the road behind us. Our eyes met. He blinked once, slowly, and I surprised myself by doing the same. He slowed the car to a crawl as we passed the pool of rosa that the animal was leaving behind.

"There," he said. "There, on the rosa."

A butterfly, yellow and black. It opened and closed. Opened and closed.

"It's drinking the rosa," said Armand.

"Is it?" I said. "How can you tell? Where is its mouth?"

I couldn't see clearly. I looked away and rubbed my eyes.

Armand in the rearview mirror, brimming with feeling.

"Round Rosa," he whispered.

He floated onto the shoulder of the highway. I stroked the handle of my only bag and closed my eyes. We came to a gentle stop in a cloud of white dust.

His eyes, textured, velvety, chenille. They never left the mirror. Armand.

He turned the car off and slumped over in the driver's seat. I took a look around. White sand for miles, tumbleweeds catching on what looked to be an ancient, exposed coral reef. In the distance, four white hills, each higher than the last, rising and rising to nothing.

"I can't go on," he said, trembling. "I can't see. I'm so sorry. This is not my day to be sad. I've had my day."

I put my bag on the floor of the car. Armand wasn't making a sound. His brown hair, electric, bristled against the ceiling. His back heaved up and down, his beautiful hands covered his face. I noticed, then, my note, folded small and wedged between his index and middle fingers.

I hesitated.

"Do you want my note?" I asked.

"No," he said, a hint of sad surprise in his voice.

"It won't work for you," I said. "My name is on it."

"I don't want your note," he said. "Of course I don't want it."

"Then—may I have it back?"

"She won't come," he said.

"My note," I said again, firmly, softly.

I saw, on the shoulder of his black denim jacket, a smear of something red, and despite my reservations, I wanted to touch it. I leaned forward and reached around the seat. My hands hovered inches above his body. I told myself: Touch, touch, set down on him.

He snapped back against his seat. My hand brushed the skin on the back of his neck. I saw him in the rearview mirror. His eyes pulsed velvet. His beat was felt. I felt it.

"Please," he said. "Do it again."

I did it again.

"And again," he said. "Harder."

And I did. Harder.

"Thank you," he said. He reached for me without turning around, his arm across his chest, his beautiful fingers waving. I let him take my hand. He pressed it. I felt the sharp corners of the note. We held the note between us.

"You should not do that," he said. "I should be doing that to you. Pressing *you* hard. You are sad. This is a sad trip for you."

"No," I said, "please don't. Please don't say anything about it."

Armand's eyes widened. The skin of them tufted up.

"Why?" he said. "Why?"

"It's very fresh," I said. "I got the news two days ago."

"Don't call it the news," said Armand. "The bowl got too deep. His heart surfaced. It came up, and he died. Your son died. His body is waiting for you to pick it up. You'll take it home.

Then you'll have to decide what to do with it. Grab onto that. Do not lose it."

He let go of me, leaving the note in my hand.

"Ophi," he said. "Ophi is dead."

"Ophi," I tried to say. "Ophi," I said again, and stumbled over the word.

Armand's eyes softened. "Ophi, Ophi, Ophi," he said. "No problem. Say it. Ophi."

I looked outside. The sun was high overhead. The hot earth was whiter than winter.

Armand took a tan parcel from the glove compartment. He opened the parcel. Inside, a high sandwich. His mouth opened wide. He took a bite. Feathered lettuce falling. Vinegar on the air. He cried as he ate, and he watched me in the rearview mirror.

"You can cry too," he said.

"I won't," I said. "I don't feel like it."

"You know what I heard recently?" he said. "*When time is steam, just cry, and the valve will open.* I think that's what I heard."

The car was warm, getting warmer.

"Let's go," I said. "Before the heat gets us."

I scanned the barren landscape. Something was missing, but what? Armand waited for me in the rearview mirror.

"The pressure is building," he said. "I have to tell you about her."

His eyes bored through me, soft, soft.

"Well," I said.

"Round Rosa," said Armand. "I rescued her from a swarm of tumbles along this very highway. I plucked her out of it. She was covered in white dust, punctured here and there, oozing little rosa. She was so grateful. She said, *Thank you, I was about to get swalled up.*"

"Swallowed," I said.

"Swalled," he said.

"Swalled."

"She let me walk her home. At her doorstep, I told her that even though we were strangers, I felt swalled up, homesick for her, and she said it was because of her shape, of her roundness, of the nest of her roundness. *We are all rolling that way*, she said.

"But I couldn't be put off. *Not me*, I insisted. *This is different.*

"I wiped my hand across her face to get the white off but underneath was more white. The little rosa smeared and made tracks.

"*You're hurt*, I said, *Let me come inside and help you.*

"Then she opened the door to her house, and I put my foot inside. She put up a little fight, but it was nothing, the door flew open, and I rushed right in. No problem.

"At first, it was hard. At dawn, I would tell her: *I worry about you. What do you do while I'm gone?*

"*But you were always gone before*, she would say. *You never were, in the beginning. And I was fine. I was fine without you.*

"*But now I am*, I would say. *Now I'm here.*

"And she would look at me, her eyes all crossed and split, and say, *But not me. I am not here. Not always. I reserve the right to be elsewhere.*

"It was I who suggested the rope. I coiled the rope at the foot of our bed. *What about it?* I asked.

"She gave me the spell to put me off (though I would not be put off for long, I was in love!). It was her gift to me, a gesture of roundness (though eventually she agreed; she had to—I was in love!).

"*If you ever want me*, she said, *when I'm not with you, say my name three times, and I'll appear.*

"*Anywhere?* I asked.

"*Anywhere*, she said. *Round Rosa, Round Rosa, Round Rosa. Just like that.*

"She was mine. I made her mine. We hiked the four hills together, the idea of the rope between us. I left my single room forever and moved into her house on the white, dusty floor of the evaporated sea.

"I was full of joy, a balloon. Our home was safe. Every surface was covered with a different, softer surface. Certain things, certain troubling things, didn't matter to me—that she did not often speak to me, that she kept a padded envelope containing a hunk of bismuth in her desk drawer, that sometimes, in certain lights, she would fade away, that she spoke on the phone to her mother in a language I'd never heard and that she would not name for me—because I felt happy.

"Sure there was the time of the paperweight and the time of the sodden beam and the time of the ceramic platter and the sunglass-smash, and, yes, there was the time of pouring my heavy stones, but she was fierce too, she was big, she had her times and those times were nothing, just nothing, to two big bodies like ours.

"Most of the time, I was happy. I was full of jokes, and Round Rosa's laughter (it escaped, it did) was like the surfacing of a hundred little hearts. (Forgive me, forgive me, it is just so apt.)

"One day I came home to find her yessing on the phone to her mother, yessing in that other language, going *pa-pa-pa-pa-pa-pa*. When she saw me there in the doorway of the kitchen, my hands stained with ink, she slammed the phone down, and with a strange look on her white face, said: *I'm pregnant.*

"In my happiness, I grabbed her, but she was not soft as she had always been, there was very little give.

"*Is this a joke?* I asked.

"She told me no, it was not a joke, it was the opposite of a joke. It was real.

"*In fact, it's more than real*, she said. *It's scrutable.*

"She lifted her shirt, and I could see a new roundness building on the old, the territory of her latest bruise growing vast. (Of course there were no times during that time. I was delicate to the extreme.)

"She grew serious. In long blue robes, she visited the doctor and returned home nodding to herself. She read books bound in onionskin that some shaking hand had signed.

"*These are rough waters*, she said when I built a wooden box-crib. *This is not a celebration.*

"The jokes dried up, but I didn't worry because at night when we lay down to sleep on our bed that was soft on soft, the idea of the rope curled up between us, and I tickled her roundness with my ink-stained fingers and left little wiggles on her skin and waved to the moon through the hole in the roof, her laughter escaped her, it did, her hundred hearts, and she smiled sometimes in her sleep.

"But in the morning there was always something. She dreamed that she'd been made flat and that vicious goats feasted on the meat of her. She moaned and lost her words. She said: *Whose moment is this?* Or: *I can't see ahead.* Or: *This can't go on.*

"*This?* I asked. *What is this?*

"*This,* she said, putting her hands on my chest and barely, just barely, pushing.

"And those two dawns, when she got loose from the idea of the rope—it wasn't escape. What would you call the sugar that slips from the bag through the hole that the hungry mouse makes? What would you call that little bit of sugar?

"Two weeks from the date, Round Rosa came home from the doctor, her robe riding high on her roundness, and put away all her books. Her mouth was small and dry. The baby was sitting up, the doctor had told her, its head tucked under her ribs. The baby was sitting on a soft wet throne inside Round Rosa.

"*They want to cut me*, she said, shrugging.

"She spent hours on the phone to her mother and would not face the moon at night. In sleep, her mouth wiggled around on her face like a worm. I was tender, or tried to be. Hear this—I put the rope, the idea of the rope, away.

"I accompanied her on the next trip to the doctor. We sat in a white office. He handed each of us a little spoon and gestured toward a bowl filled with powder. Round Rosa filled her spoon and dropped it. The powder drifted toward the floor. She tried to bend to reach it but could not get past her roundness. She struggled.

"*Stop it*, I said, more sharply than I'd intended. *Leave it.*

"She squinted at me as if I were a barely discernible thing advancing toward her through the night.

"I set my spoon on the doctor's desk and pointed it at Round Rosa.

"*Is it absolutely necessary?* I asked.

"*It is*, said the doctor, a tall man in black boots. *These sorts of babies can only be sliced into life. It's just a quick stab, a sharp drag, a fleshy yawn. Then—boom! Baby.*

"Round Rosa. Her hands folded in her lap. Her head bowed. I could not look away from her roundness, my melon in the stream, the body of our bodies.

"*That can't be true*, I said.

"The doctor stood up. *Would you argue with a baby?* he asked. *Baby knows best.*

"*But the baby has already made one mistake*, I said. *The baby is sitting up.*

"*So? The baby is king! Listen*, said the doctor, tapping his head. *It is now after lunchtime. Do you understand?*

"Round Rosa interjected. *We understand*, she said.

"*Good!* he said, winking at her. *The baby wants this. It is best for the baby if we cut you. Don't be afraid of a little rosa.*

"*I'm not*, said Round Rosa. She turned to me. *Please don't argue*, she said. *Please don't hold me back.*

"I had nothing to say. We followed the doctor down a maze of identical corridors to the sea-blue doors of the operating room. The doctor flung the doors open on an operation-in-progress—the place was the size of a tennis court. Seven men in green stood over a body, a body draped in green, and the equipment, the massive equipment, it, too, was draped in green, and the rosa sprayed up and spattered the men. The doctor laughed. *Oops*, he said, laughing. *It's really quite safe*, and Round Rosa, for the first time in our life together, reached for my hand. *She* for *me*.

"The operation was set. We had one week. I did a great deal of reading. Then, late one night, I happened upon a hopeful piece of information.

"*The baby can be flipped!* I told her, expecting excitement. I begged her to try. I gave her a list of tasks. *Stand on your head*, I said. *Shroud your little toe in smoke, breathe on a plank, be like a crow and then a dog and then a crow again—hypnotize your roundness. Kick the baby off its throne!*

"But Round Rosa was resigned.

"*They need to cut me*, she offered, as if I had not heard. *These sorts of babies can only be sliced into life.*

"She spent most of the week sitting at the kitchen table holding a broom. Her mother called, but Round Rosa would not come to the telephone. I tried to explain to her mother in the simplest terms: *She is not sweeping. But she wants to sweep. She is not busy, but she wants to be. Do you understand? I can't make her sweep. I can't make her come to the phone.* But her mother didn't understand. *Ehn*, she said, *ehn, ehn, ehn*, and hung up.

"The day came. Round Rosa, prepped for surgery, on a gurney. Her roundness, bare, painted a dark orange, poked up through a green sheet, my melon in the stream, the body of our bodies. Her hair tucked away beneath more green. Her face—white, whiter.

"She reached for me for the second time. She pressed my hand. I opened completely. I unfolded. Every bit of me could be seen. She was trembling. But was she afraid? Her eyes sparkled with mischief.

"*Remember*, I said. *Only the spirit can split you.*

"She smiled, she was not right. She mumbled, I leaned down close.

"*I'm gonna*, she said, *split.* And the doctor rolled her through the swinging doors.

"*You can watch through the window*, the doctor said, *but only when the doors have stopped swinging. When the doors stop swinging—then, feast your eyes.*

"Round Rosa.

"I waited.

"I remembered the spell. I believed in the spell. She'll come, I told myself. Even if.

"The swinging stopped. The window in the door began to glow. I looked in.

"I saw this—

"(Believe me. Believe me.)

"A field in the moonlight, silver, gold and gray. Round Rosa, nude, on a wooden cart. Round Rosa, her roundness surrounded, on the bed of the cart. Round Rosa, clean in flowers, led by horses. Two women in the field. Two women in black. One with a wooden bowl, one with a knife. They climbed onto the bed of the cart. They knelt in flowers, blue and green. Round Rosa anointed by moonlight, her roundness bathed in silver and gold and gray. All hands on her roundness, all eyes. One woman raised the knife. The other held the bowl. Round Rosa buried her head in flowers. Her roundness rose.

"I tapped on the window in the door. The women froze like animals.

"*Let me in*, I yelled. *I'm the father. Round Rosa!*

"I pushed on the doors, but they would not move. They saw that I could not come, and smiled. But Round Rosa, headless in the flowers—what did she see? What did she want?

"One woman cut her wide. Her roundness opened. I saw the body of our bodies, held aloft by the other, dangling over the sunken nest of Round Rosa's roundness. Then rosa, rosa everywhere. Roundness rosa, flowers rosa. Rosa in the wooden bowl. Rosa overcoming the bowl. Rosa on the muscle of horse. Rosa over field. Sea of rosa. Wave of rosa against the glass. Rosa, rosa, over all."

THE HEAT IN THE CAR WAS EXTREME. ARMAND SAT LOW in the driver's seat, his mouth open. His fingers were curled up around his palms, which had turned purple in the sun. I reached forward to touch him and burned my arm on the back of the leather seat.

"What happened?" I asked.

"She disappeared," he said. "Round Rosa and the body of our bodies. It was rosa over all and then nothing. I called for her. I called for the body of our bodies. But no one came. I must have collapsed. Someone moved me. I was moved. I woke up the next day at home in bed next to Round Rosa's rumpled robe. I found the doctor, and he claimed never to have met me. I called her mother but ehn, ehn, ehn."

"We need water," I said. "We're exhausted."

Armand caught me in the rearview mirror, his eyes lumpy and defiant, his hair afloat. "I can't live," he said, "without her body."

"There was no field," I snapped, I was so hot. "No women in black. No cart."

Armand shook his head. His eyes, in the mirror, pitied me.

"There *was* a field," he said. "It was rosa over field. Rosa over all."

Sweat ran into my eyes. Sweat sprang from the crease of my elbow. The note was damp. I unfolded it and read it again. There was my name in capital letters. Then: *The bearer of this note is the father of the body. The bearer of this note can travel freely.*

"Armand," I said.

"I won't go," he said, his eyes flashing.

I could not tell how long we'd been sitting. The white highway shimmered in the midday sun. I looked for the half-crushed animal, but it had disappeared into the dust. The pool of its rosa boiled in the sun. The butterfly was gone, but where last it had stood, on the skin of the pool of rosa, a bubble was forming.

"Look," I said. "Look. Armand."

He pressed his beautiful hands, his forehead, against the car window. It must have burned, but he did not flinch.

Together, we watched the bubble grow and grow. Its skin was opaque, brilliant, cardinal-red.

Armand opened the car door and walked toward the rosa.

"She won't come," I said from behind the glass. "She won't. That's not her."

"Round Rosa," said Armand, covering his eyes.

"Round Rosa," he said again.

I got out of the car. I went to him. We stood on opposite sides of the pool. "I've been afraid to try," he said. "I've been afraid to go for three."

He opened his arms.

"Round Rosa!" he cried. "Round Rosa! Round Rosa!"

Heavy, hot silence. The boiling of the rosa, the gurgle and pop.

"Armand," I said.

For a moment it looked as if he might attack me. He came toward me around the pool, his arms extended monstrously. I let him come. He wrapped his beautiful fingers, his lovely fronds, around my neck but did not squeeze. His heart came through to his fingertips and pulsed against me.

"Is it too tight?" he said, leaning in, squeezing.

I collapsed into him, my wet nose on his wet neck.

"No," I told him. "No. I could get free, if I wanted to."

ARMAND AND I SAID OUR GOODBYES AT THE RESEARCH hospital.

"Get the body," he said. "Grab onto it. Seize it, what is yours."

"Of course," I told him. "Yes."

I was taken to the family lounge. An old woman slept on a cot in the corner, her feathered hat covering her face. I was told by the yellow-handed undertaker that the body had spontaneously sublimed just one hour earlier while laid out on the presenting table, a not uncommon occurrence in cases where the bowl had become so deep as to show the heart.

"We're sorry you missed it," said the undertaker. "We know what the body means."

"You can linger," he said. "Compose yourself. Take time, but not too much."

I made sure the old woman was asleep. I touched her soft neck, and she made no sign. I pushed the cot through the swinging door and into the dark hallway and came back into the lounge alone. I sat on the floor in the center of the room.

I slapped my own rough hand. I squeezed my own coarse neck. I sobbed. The undertaker returned and pointed at the clock. "We're sorry," he said. "But, as we said—"

I moved to the far corner of the room. "Just a little longer," I said.

The undertaker frowned. "Not here," he said. "Not inside. There is no little longer here."

"But this," I said, "is where the body was."

"But the body is not," said the undertaker. "It is not."

He pointed to the clock. He waved a yellow finger.

"Ophi," I said, without wanting.

"Ophi," I said, but no.

"Ophi," I said, but did not deserve.

The undertaker frowned. "We know what the body means. But the body is gone. It won't come back. The body is, as they say, on the air."

"Armand!" I said, getting up off the ground.

"Armand!" I said, my rough match.

"Armand!" I said again, this time with hope, and guess who came running through the door?

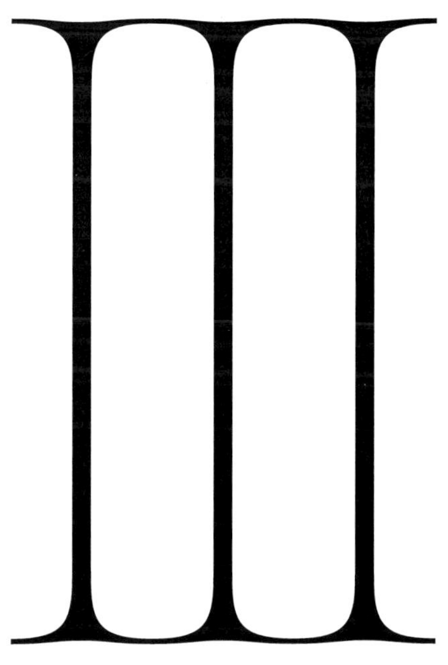

The End of
the Party

As usual, I was unimpressed with Don Meeko's wife. She was livid, pinched, and silent, and despite having nothing interesting to say about the documentary film we had just watched, she had chosen to occupy the most central position in the drawing room.

Her hair was the centerpiece. She wore it mussed, as if from an all-day sex trial.

Tony, who had lost his money, sipped his imitation tea. He was irritable. Of the six of us, he was the only one who had expected to enjoy the film.

"I didn't think they would show the actual bodies. I don't know what I thought they *would* show. Reenactments, I guess. Their possessions. I'm no filmmaker, but I know what a film should do."

Tony had two hands, but he only ever used one. The teacup was a bit too heavy but he refused to correct himself. Usually,

I forgave him for this. I thought of it as an aesthetic constraint. But here, on the tail of the film I had just endured, I saw his refusal for what it was: propaganda.

"And what's that?" I asked. "What is it that a film should do?"

Tony's wife Camille was crowding the French doors.

"Don't answer, Antonio," she said sweetly. "He's baiting you. The truth is he's a slave to his squeamishness just like the rest of us."

"I see that you're trying to blinker me, Camille," replied Tony. His tea sloshed ruthlessly. It escaped to darken his crotch. "A film should comfort" (and here he paused, he was criminally unsure) "a film should correct. The camera should not linger on dead bodies in the surf."

"You want the coast to be clear?" said Don Meeko, and everyone groaned.

Don Meeko's wife seeped a single word. "Stupid," she said through her nose. I waved my hand around to show how much she stunk. But I knew she would not give up her position in the center of the room. I had been at this party before.

Tony, above the clatter of his cup, pushed ahead. "The camera should show us the beds that the bodies fled before they became bodies. The beds of war. It should show us where the bodies slept so that we realize how little home can offer when there's violence about."

My wife was somewhere, enough to later count as having been in attendance. During the opening credits of the film, she'd whispered to me: *Oh! I think I know this director… psychically.*

"Irina," I had responded, "you and I are not quarantined inside of this conversation. Are you aware of that? This theater is a home theater and it is quite small and everyone can hear you, so please shut up."

Predictably, when the film ended, Irina had not come into the drawing room with everyone else. Perhaps she was still in the home theater. Perhaps the pantry. But what did I care where she was so long as she was quiet?

Outside on the patio, a book lay open on a big wooden table. The wind blew through its pages and something red—a graceful little pip of color, a piece of paper with great heart—rose out of the book's middle and briefly rode the breeze and then fell on the flagstone, where it shivered, its sides curling up.

Don Meeko, fat with gold buttons down his chest, moved Camille from her position in front of the French doors (she resisted, that plank). Then he went through to the outside, closing the doors behind him—as if there could be privacy from us—and stalked across the patio.

Beyond his great shoulder was the silver river made depthless by the sun. The gentle hump of its bank was like the lustful lip of the vast green countryside. Don Meeko hung in the foreground, swaying over the little red slip of paper. Then to prove that he was our host and could do anything, he stomped the paper beneath his boot, ground it with his heel, and finally snatched it up, thrusting it deep into the pocket of his vest that usually held his cigarettes.

Tony set his shaking teacup on a waist-high table and went on talking as if the scene on the patio had not happened. "Worst of all," Tony said, "was the close-up of the wound."

"Oh, I didn't look," said Camille. She was fingering a dried rosebud that hung from the ceiling on a length of twisted twine. "I couldn't look. I knew it would be too real."

Don Meeko's wife rolled her eyes. It seemed to me that her hair had been recently heaved. It stubbornly held its interior. I counted the number of entrances into it—there were at least seven. Naturally, and grossly, I thought of Don Meeko and his role in it, but when I looked for him on the patio, he was no longer there.

"It was," said Tony. "It was too real, but it also made no sense. They drowned. Why should there have been a wound in a body at all? A body drowns in order to escape violence. Drowning is what killed them. The wound misleads. The wound is beside the point."

Don Meeko came in through the library. "Use your imagination, Tony," he bellowed. He was carrying a tray of drinks. Violet-colored. Petaled glasses.

"Lover?" He offered the tray to his wife. She closed her eyes and turned her head. Said nothing. Don Meeko moved on, smiling vaguely.

Her behavior disturbed me. Her refusal—it too was propaganda. How had I never noticed before? I wondered about Irina but did not think of going to find her. I had become aware of the possibility of boredom, so I committed myself more completely to the conversation.

"The wound," I said, "could have come from anything. The bodies had been in the water for a long time, so the wound could have been a nibble, some sea-thing taking a bite, or the body could have come up against a bit of ocean-trash, something ragged, made of metal, sharp enough to rip the flesh, which was probably fairly soft, the flesh, from soaking, if we're being real, but anyway what does it matter what happens to a body after it's dead? You know, this is what's wrong with the film. We watched it, the whole thing, and now we're thinking about the wound instead of the war. We're concerned not with the persons left behind in the beds of war, who are sleeping *inside of war* right this second, but with the corpses that escaped. There are reasons to film the living instead of the dead. The wound is not a portal. Neither is the mouth of a corpse. They don't offer us transport. Why show them at all?"

"But isn't a bed?" said Camille, in a needling tone. "A bed is a portal, isn't it?"

I was on the verge of a rant, but I noticed that Don Meeko's wife appeared to be listening to me, and I did not want to please her by losing control. She twirled a ratty bit of hair around her finger, which was very thin, though her knuckles were swollen and red. I stood and moved toward the center of the room. As I approached, she lifted her dress very slightly and showed her shoes. She wore a strange sort of boot whose laces began at the tip of the shoe and traveled a narrow path up to and past the ankle. Her feet were monstrously long, perhaps as long as my forearm, and I drew back at the sight of them.

"What did you think of the wound?" I asked, looking through the French doors to the world beyond.

Don Meeko's wife blinked slowly. Her eyes were unfocused and dim. "What did I think of the wound?" She shrugged. "It looked like an invitation… an erotic one."

Tony bowed his head. He looked deep into his imitation tea. Camille moved stiffly across the room toward her husband. When she reached him, she did not stay but, performing a fresh interest in the hanging flower she had just left, returned to the dried bud and rolled it around between her fingers as if seeing it for the first time.

"So elegant," she said. "Even with all this dust."

Don Meeko clapped his hands. "It's that time of the afternoon," he said, "when I must remind us of how long our nights tend to go. Let's nap."

IRINA WAS NOT IN OUR BEDROOM, BUT THERE WERE traces of her everywhere: Her pink and puffy clutch sat like a pound of flesh on the nightstand, the acrid melon-sweet smell of her urine lingered in the bathroom. Carelessly, she'd left her secret reading open on the bed: *You Must Try* by Dr. H. M. Trot.

I flopped onto my back and read a few lines: *Even if a full release would seem to threaten the integrity of the entrance, it must still be attempted. A rip is preferred to a repression. Take, for example, the case of the woman who spent all her time in the stables…*

I tossed the book against the wall and rolled onto my side. I tried for sleep but was pestered by thoughts of Don Meeko's wife and her preposterous hair—a trap! a labyrinth! a deflection! Clearly, I had been wounded by it, but I was not sure why. Before closing my eyes, I resolved to wake before the appointed time so as to beat her to the center of the drawing room. I would take her seat and keep it for the rest of the night's activities so as not to be forced, by the fact of her prime placement, to consider her.

A SHORT TIME LATER, I BOLTED AWAKE. THE WINDOW glowed golden and rose. It was not quite evening, which meant I still had a chance. I bounded down the stairs, feeling hopeful. But when I entered the drawing room, Don Meeko's wife was already there. Perhaps she had not moved. Her eyes were dark and sagging.

"Good evening," I said.

"I hope it will be," she said. The tips of her extra-long feet stuck out from beneath the hem of her skirt like the heads of two sinister eels.

The rest of the guests filtered into the room. Tony's face wore the crease of his pillow. Camille carried a large green ledger tucked up beneath her stickish arm. Don Meeko entered last. He sipped from an aluminum canteen; his lips were stained cherry red. "I don't know about you," he said, "but that nap returned me to my optimism, and I don't want to hear another word about the film."

Everyone nodded their agreement, except for Don Meeko's wife, who was engaged in the difficult activity of turning her chair around without standing up. She gripped the arms of the chair and, little by little, jumping and jerking, her hair quivering but never collapsing, she managed to turn herself toward the patio and the silver river beyond.

Camille sighed. "I love this time of night," she said. She wandered through the golden glow toward the French doors. She held her hands around a tiny fluttering nothing. I could see the beating of this nothing travel up through her forearm, through what little flesh she had. "I know it's obvious of me, but I used to go outside when I was a girl. Back then there were reasons that had nothing to do with men. Reasons to be alone and to do things…"

When Camille had almost reached the doors, Don Meeko's wife stood up and began to scream. The sound was inorganic. Industrial. I covered my ears. She pointed past Camille, past the patio, to the greater outside. "A child," she cried. "A child was standing on the riverbank. And now I don't see him. He's fallen in. I don't see him anywhere at all."

Don Meeko rushed to her side and tried to pin her down. "Lover," he said. "Don't get up. Why would there be a child? We don't know any children."

She shook him off, then turned to me. Gave me a withering look. "If he can't, what about you?" she said. "Can you overcome yourself? Can you leave the party? A child is drowning."

I'd never been given such explicit permission, and now I jumped at the chance to leave, however briefly. I pushed through the French doors, took the patio in three steps and ran through the ornamental garden, kicking pebbles here and there. I stepped off the lawn and into the high grass. I felt happy out there without them. My knees were warm. They were following after me, I knew they would be, but I could no longer hear them.

The riverbank was sodden. The sand, dark. The river flowed swiftly along, and I accepted its disregard as a matter of course.

The others arrived. Tony was out of breath. He bent at the waist and spat. Camille held back, stayed in the field. The grass was up to her waist. Her torso floated along the horizon of grass and sky. Don Meeko's wife advanced toward the water and Don Meeko grabbed at her skirt as it dragged through the wet dark sand.

"Here," she said. "Look."

The water had nearly erased them, but they were still undeniably there: two tiny footprints.

She turned to Don Meeko. "I'm your wife," she said. "And a child has fallen into the river."

He screwed up his face. His fingers battled his run of gold buttons. He removed his vest, went to the water's edge, and flopped stomach-first into the river. He sank beneath the silvery impenetrable surface of the water. For the first time in years, we were without a host.

Tony pranced around. He looked thrilled. "He can't swim," he said, and Camille, who was laughing, said, "It's true. He doesn't even know how to float!"

"Well," said Don Meeko's wife. "He must try."

I went in after him. He was there, just below the surface, lying motionless in the current, but I could not lift him up. I slid my hands down the length of his arms and found his fists anchored wrist-deep in the river bottom. He was holding on. I kicked his wrists until he let go, and when I lifted his head out of the water, his eyes were wistful and his teeth were chattering. He would not look at his wife but took some time lying on the shore before reaching, with trembling hands, for the gold buttons on his crumpled vest.

The mood was dark. I offered to investigate the riverbank until darkness fell.

"There's no point now," said Don Meeko's wife. In the dusky light, her hair seemed to consist not of strands but of a single mass onto which someone had drawn a series of experimental revolutions. She brought two fingers to her forehead and pressed. Though I had not thought her capable of it, she did, in some practiced way, seem upset.

"We missed the window," she said. "And I, for one, won't cling to the idea of the child's survival."

Not wanting to go back inside, I stayed to search. I waded downriver, picking my way over many submerged roots. I passed a fenced pasture, a bathtub full of trash, and two tipping gravestones that faced the river. *Otho Woods*, read one. *Otho Woods*, read the other.

When true night hit, I quickly caught a chill. As I slopped through the grass back toward the house, I said her name as a test: "Irina. Irina. Irina."

THE DRAWING ROOM WAS LIVELY. THEY WERE PLAYING A game of Gesture, which Don Meeko was clearly winning. But his wife was nowhere to be found. The central chair was empty. And Irina, it was just as well, was not there either.

I stood shivering in the French doors, unsure of whether or not to remove my shoes. Beneath the dangling rose, the little red paper sat crumpled on the floor. It had escaped the considerable depth of Don Meeko's pocket some time prior to his plunge. I pried off my wet shoes and padded across the carpet. I crouched behind the couch and smoothed out the paper. It was a list of the names of everyone in attendance. Next to Irina's name, there was a question mark. Next to Don Meeko's wife, a star.

I stood up, shivering even more. "There's a fire in the library," said Don Meeko, still gesturing hard. "I'm burning all the aromatics in the house. We've had such a hard evening. Please, go get warm."

FOR A LONG TIME, I STARED DOWN THE HALLWAY, unable to decide to go. The library was the place of my first meeting with Irina. We had both just arrived for a long weekend at Don Meeko's. Right away, we were introduced to his new and mysterious bride, and later that night, before the empty fireplace, we had guessed back and forth about her:

I hear she is critically ill.

I heard she was involved in the Lady's Day Bombing.

Me too, I heard that too, but she looks too young.

Do you think she's lively enough for him? Will she know the right games?

Do you think… have you noticed… that she looks a bit like me?

But this evening, the library was different. It was filled with a noxious cloud of burning aromatics. Don Meeko's wife sat alone by the fire, her back to me, so that she did not notice my arrival. She was sitting in a plush but armless chair, her chin against her chest. Her long and curious shoes were drying on the hearth. I lingered in the doorway as she raised her skirt and settled it across her thighs. Then she propped her left ankle on her right knee and began to tend to her foot. Her very little foot.

It was a foot that made no sense on a woman. It was short and squat, lacking form. The sole of it had no waist. It was a child's foot, and its bottom was dark with dirt. Don Meeko's wife dampened her skirt with spit and began to wipe the dirt away.

I looked again at her extra-long boots. Without anything in them, they had curled into something resembling the discarded skin of a snake. Slowly, silently, I left the library. I rushed through the house, looking for Irina. She was not in the pantry or the cellar or the private museum. I remembered the basement bathrooms. I knew they sealed totally, and she liked to be shut up. I descended the cold cement stairs and inhaled deeply. Nothing. I returned to the drawing room, which was now empty. I tried the kitchen and had begun to think of going outside, where she most certainly would not be, when I saw a darkness floating behind the frosted glass of the conservatory door.

"Irina," I whispered.

Yes. I'm here.

"Come out."

I can't, my love. I'm marching for a cause.

"You're alone in a room," I said. The doorknob was stuck. I thought of breaking the frosted glass.

It's so beautiful, she replied. *You can't imagine. We are one large woman who has dressed to please herself.*

"Irina, you are alone in a room at Don Meeko's."

There are no men here. There are not even children. I feel like a mountain.

"Come out," I pleaded. "Let's go home. I'm tired of being a guest. And besides, the party's over."

I won't. I'll march instead. Against tyranny in every form. Don't wait for me.

"We must go. There's a game afoot. One we have not agreed to play."

We hold hands. We link arms. We aren't at all shy about touching. It's so beautiful, you can't imagine. No art. No war. No marriage. No party.

"Irina," I said, making one last attempt. "You're alone in there, and you're lonely. Please come out."

No. It's so beautiful. You can't imagine what it is to be a mountain. But try, my love. For me. You must try.

Neftali

Before Neftali came, the grounds of her husband's estate had cowered under her care. She'd grown dandelions, crabgrass, little orange trees choked out by the dust. After Neftali, the world outside was monstrous: wide lawns, towering trees, flat-faced flowers. This pleased her, as she could walk around feeling equal to nature. Singular gardener. He would not defer to the limits of climate, not to God, not even to her.

When she hired him, in the moment of sealing the deal, Neftali pressed his lips against her clammy palms, and she saw the curtain lift to show the stage she'd set for herself—the lifelessness of a modern column, the idiocy of an arch, the lameness of a library where 100 men could read and where each could think: Only I am reading. Life took place outside! She'd known it once and now she could know it again.

"What do you envision?" she asked Neftali on his first day, gesturing to the scrub, and he answered, "An allée of cypress, long as my nights. A limestone wellhead, a pleasure pool."

Pleasure was the last car of the train. She had given it up, but all this time it had been coming. Now she looked up from her reading. Now she saw the end in sight.

She met Neftali each morning in the courtyard, where he would whisper: "How would you like the garden to sound? Like this" (and a breath), "or like this" (and a finer breath). "Like this," she might say, and sigh and remove her hat. "Or like this," and press her tongue to her teeth and buzz and take his wrist.

Once, she carried a hard stool into the garden, still not sure how to take advantage of her leisure, and perched on it trying to read in the heat. She could hear, but not see, the water steps that Neftali had made for her. The sound of the water contained her voice and the voices of several interesting men in conversation. A headless thrill passed through her: Elsewhere in that very same garden, Neftali was hard at work, while she was hardly living, softly chatting with a bevy of vague and gurgling men, and this, thanks to him, could be the case whenever she wanted.

The massive plants that kept her hidden from her children—these were his monsters. She, too, was one—she relaxed while he labored to grow a home for her free time. And somewhere nearby he was sweating through his shirt—the thought tore through her like anger. Tender of her life, immodest to the extreme. He had become indispensable. Oh, awful need!

Soon she would ask him to move two large chairs out into the garden, then the vase of peacock feathers, then the table she liked best for peeling fruit, then the one she liked for drawing. Then she would ask him to sit with her, and he would pretend to resist, and she would finally say, "I need you to sit," and only then would he sit, and take a blueberry from the mound, and hold it in his sticky fingers, and offer it to her, slipping everything (berry, knuckles, sweat) into her mouth. And afterward he might say, "I don't care what you do when you're not with me."

And suddenly nothing else mattered. She thought only of him. But she made no effort to stop it beyond that of noticing, neutrally, each instant of her feeling as it developed.

Near the border of her husband's estate, Neftali grew a monstrous pyracantha, a wall of thorn, dense with its small, red fruit, to shield his gardener's quarters from view. Now and then, she walked along the hedge, catching her dress on the bunches of berries, parting the leaves—why not? It belonged to her, though she'd not yet tested this boundary. She knew there were sisters living with him in his quarters, and a poor, pale mother, all breathing behind the hedge, all alive and living with him in his meager home, a home he left each morning to come to her.

One day, she came to the end of the hedge, and she waffled there, asking herself, Will I look? Will I not look? Until she took a step toward looking and ran into Neftali, who was steaming, who was gripping a bag of worms.

"Why are you here," he said, leading her along the hedge up the green slope to her massive home. "I was coming to you. I always do."

She saw the worms swirl against the side of his bag, and she lied: "I'm hurt. Perhaps I'm ill. I've eaten one of these berries."

A darkness, his scorn, passed between them. "No," he said, pinching a berry, "these are only bitter, not poisonous. Is it the flu?"

"No, I'm cool, I'm even."

"An allergy?"

"I have none."

"Something's troubling you."

"I can't say."

He led her across the great lawn. "Lie down," he said, and she lowered herself onto a wicker chaise near the hibiscus.

"Stay awhile," she said.

"I can't. No."

He picked a yellow, trumpeting blossom and turned it around between his fingers.

"Stay," she said.

He smiled. "You don't need me. You need some rest."

She closed her eyes. "I need you to stay," she said.

The grass was wet, but he knelt there, one hand on his bag as if it were a treasured pet.

"Let's play a game," he said.

"I'd like to."

"I'm missing something. Guess what it is."

She propped herself up on her elbows. "Okay, "she said.

He stretched out to his full length and rolled onto his side in the grass. "Take a look," he said.

She looked. She began at his feet and traveled the length of his pants, whose true color she could not tell. She lingered over his stomach, the circle of sweat around his neck.

"Is it a real thing?" she asked.

"Yes. Very real. I lost it a long time ago."

"When did you last see it?"

"I was so young."

"Do you think of it?"

"Hardly ever."

"Is it a common thing?"

"That depends."

"On?"

He smiled. "Do you like this game?"

She looked at the sun and then at him. He was the color of the deep end, where she once preferred to swim. Her eyes played tricks with his body—one blue arm ending in a point, a long and wild hair of blue, a deeper and deeper blue spreading from his head to his neck and so on and so on. She was on her way down.

"I do," she said. "I like it."

"Keep guessing," he said. "It belonged to my body."

"Belonged?"

"Yes, I once had it."

"Do you miss what is missing?"

"I'm not sure. I couldn't say. I've only ever been without."

"Tonsils?"

"Lower."

"A toe?"

"Higher."

"Where?"

He stood up. "Where do you think?"

"Stop," she said. "Stay." And she reached for him.

He brought her the yellow hibiscus flower and pushed its powdered tip against her cheek. He said, "You've seen what I'm missing. You like me just fine without."

"Oh," she said, blushing happily. "That. Yes."

He swung his bag of worms over his shoulders and walked away, and she tried not to, she tried, she clenched her teeth to keep from it, but she could not help herself—she cried out for him: "Don't go."

But he went. She thought she heard her children and sat up straight, smoothed her dress over her throbbing lap as if to make a place for a tray, but it was only the sound of the newest fountain, gloomy Neptune surveying his green sea. Cruel gardener. She shrank away from his vast lawn, his paddled leaves.

She recalled her first years on the estate, when she and her husband had run dry dusty races against the children. Back then, it was dirt and shrubs. The rooms were without furniture, and they would throw themselves on the cool tile floor, having sprinted all the way up from the ocean, and her husband would reach across the coolness and pinch her elbow. They had not yet visited Switzerland. They had not met and lost the famous children's author. They had not entertained a single guest. Their favorite pastime was to watch the horizon through a large telescope. The children, especially. Her husband liked to tell them that a giant grape was rolling toward them across the ocean and that some night, a night when they'd failed to keep watch, it would hit and they would all wake up in jelly. This was how it was, before.

Her husband's growth, at first, was just a roughness, a smear like coffee grounds on his cheek, but it grew to obscure his left eye and half of his nose. Eventually, it wiped out the borders of his mouth. She begged him to do as the doctor said. She thrust his children onto his lap. "These children belong to you!" she screamed. But he had not been moved, not once. When she dropped to her knees, when she whipped herself with his belt, when she hit her head against the silver tray, he would simply bow to her. He would bow and say the few inadequate sentences that were soon to become her idea of a husband: "I see your anger and your sadness. I honor your feeling. But above all, I honor my own. I desire freedom. I desire it excessively. I will have it."

At some point she stopped struggling. Some vigilance sloughed off. She no longer counted her children in their heavy sleigh beds at night.

Now, as she lay throbbing in the glow of Neftali's game, her husband appeared in the garden. He almost never left the library, not having the health for it, but he had come to her anyway, wrapped in a plaid blanket, wetting his slippers on the grass. She tried not to look at him so that his growth would not register.

"The garden is high," he said. "Neftali's been hard at work."

"Why are you out? The doctor advised against it."

"Only you have seen the doctor. I have not. I am not subject to her advice, or her reality."

"How's the reading going?" she asked.

"I did come for a reason, love. My brother's been watching you from La Casetta. He says you glide around all day, sitting, resting, peeling fruit. He says you seem bored. Are you?"

"I'm enjoying the garden. Has he fixed the big tear in his robe?"

"You're in need of spiritual refreshment," he said. "I can feel it, too."

"I don't see how you could."

He smiled. "I haven't forgotten you," he said. They stared at each other like twins with amnesia. "We've broken ground on the upper plot," he said. "Soon, we'll begin work on the glass chapel. My desire—my exceptional desire—is that you take charge of the chapel grounds. You and Neftali. Will you? Design and plan and execute? You need a little project, I think."

He pointed up the hillside to where a patch of brush had been cleared. A few giant machines, elegant and prehistoric, were poised to begin work on the naked allotment.

She thought of the hours they would spend together in this other unoccupied area, clear of her children, his sisters, his poor, pale mother. "Sure," she said. "If you like."

ON THE DAY NEFTALI FELL, THEY HAD LUNCHED together on the border of the triangular fountain. It had just begun to flow, and she kept taking little sips from it until Neftali grabbed her wrist and shook the water from her hands.

"Are you trying to make yourself sick?"

"No."

"Idiot," he said, and she shrugged. And then he knelt down, as he had never done before, he laid his head on her lap, and he sighed. "There's something wrong with you," he said. "Something is missing."

"Oh no," she said, trying to laugh like a bunny in a cartoon. "I'm fine."

Somewhere a bridge refused to lower, though she so desperately watched the other side. Neftali pulled her to her feet, then led her to the pile of tile, the azure diamonds they'd selected, together, for their unusual shape and their radiance.

"Where do you think these should go?" he asked.

She spun around, letting her arms move however they would move.

"Oh, who cares. These should line the path through the rose garden," she said. "It might be nice. It might make people feel like they were following a private river."

"Listen to what I'm going to do instead," he said. "I'm not going to do what you suggest. I'm going to lay these tiles on the roof over the stone walk. The roof will be feathered in blue. You're going to wait in the chapel while I work—no matter how long I work. You are allowed to watch me through the glass, but you are not allowed to interrupt. When I'm done, you will meet me in the organ room."

She felt as if she'd been put to bed by the largest hands in the world. She nodded yes, and he glared at her. "This is no ritual violence," he said, "visited on the weak. This is what you want me to do."

"Yes," she said. "Yes, I know."

The plan was to surround the chapel with redwoods so that one day the glass walls would disappear and become the forest, but at first the trees were young and short and the sun beat down and beat down on the wooden pews and on the stone pulpit and on the top of her head as she sat there emptying her mind. Her husband had desired that the place be outside of the world, and though she could see what he was after, she could not say to herself that her husband was kind or noble or fair or that she knew him, in the end.

As she sat there, she thought of her father wearing a white nightgown, astride a large black horse, leading a cavalry charge up the hill to the chapel. He held a rifle at his side, and he yelled to his bugler, *Make me known to her once more!*

When Neftali fell, she was watching. She saw him slip from the roof of the long covered walk. He fell with style and with power, as only he could do. She was inside and he was out, but the day was still—she thought she could hear him land. Boosh. Then the tile came down in blue shards, like ice chipped off the moon.

From where she sat watching, on that piney pew in the glass chapel, the fall seemed staged. She almost laughed. Almost, despite her children who thought only of skiing, her brother-in-law who wore shredded silk, and her husband who refused the cure. Almost, but that she knew Neftali's worth. She had often watched him climb the 15-foot sprinkler he'd built to unlock her garden, never fearing for his safety, and she could not stand to lose a single one of her beliefs.

But now Neftali had fallen from the roof of the long covered walk. Yes, she had almost laughed to see it, but hadn't he, too, grinned at her before dropping out of sight, as if to let her know he would be okay? Or had he meant something else by grinning? She imagined his landing, salty skin stuck fast to the azure tile. No blood, only the blue of an orderly mosaic laid neatly around him by some other, greater worker, as if to decorate his error—as if error were part of his architecture.

Yes, he had fallen. And they had smiled at each other through the glass. Some time had passed, but she had not moved from her pew, and he had not reappeared upon the roof. She was thinking things over. She waited long enough for concern to tip the scale, and then she stepped outside. But a stranger stood in her way. He was wearing a robe that may once have been black but was now a non-color that told of the length and severity of his exposure. He wore his hair in a neat bowl with one thin braid hanging down, beginning somewhere behind his left ear.

"Excuse me," she said. She tried to see past him to Neftali, but the angle wouldn't allow.

"Good morning," he said. "Can I ask you something? Do you need me?"

She shook her head.

"Let me start again—I can perform certain spiritual duties. It looks like you might need me."

"I don't understand."

"I was walking by—I've come a long way—and I saw this unusual structure. This wooden skeleton of a chapel. But then the sun caught the glass. Glass-walled! How unusual, I thought, and what does it mean? And how can I help?"

She felt as if she'd unwittingly got into a maelstrom with him, that the two of them were circling a point inside of which everything would vanish.

"We don't need help," she said.

"Is this a chapel?"

"Yes."

"And has a priest been assigned?"

"No."

"I require almost nothing."

"Please excuse me, someone has fallen."

"I've lived my whole life in the sun, is there not a place for me here?"

"A worker. He may be hurt."

"Did you hear me?"

"I must get by."

"Did you hear how little I require?"

"That's not the problem."

"What is the problem?"

"A worker is hurt."

"Can I help? I'm destined to."

"Let me pass."

"No," he said. "I say no."

She tried to push past, but he was firm. He held her wrist.

"I'll let you go, but not before I've told you something."

He bent down to meet her height, to show that he was serious. She gave up.

"Yes, okay," she said, "I see."

"When I was a boy, I had a pony named K. My family was poor, so you might guess that K wasn't a present. She was an accident. We lived in an old shipping container that sat by the sea. It was my office, then, to gather grasses (my mother made baskets to sell) and all day I would gather these grasses, sometimes until I lost feeling in my fingers or fell asleep and woke up choking on sand. But I didn't think: Poor me. I understood my usefulness. And as I got older and began to suffer under *la luxure*, the hard work struck a balance. Every day I advanced sincerely as a child, I had no desires that were not tempered by the outdoors. And then one day, as I took a rest in the grass and ate my lunch of beans, I felt the wind begin to trace me as if nature were making a blueprint for my body, and I readied myself for something wild, for revelation or sensual synthesis, and just as I felt it might arrive, just as I felt that I would have to face up to life, a pony appeared.

"Beautiful pony, the color of milk spilled onto caramel. She was curious, but reserved. I offered her a fistful of grass, which she took from me, turning so I could not watch her eat. Eventually, she let me touch her, and I took her blonde mane in my hands and ran it across my own neck. What a feeling. I got quite close. We got quite close, the two of us. I named her K, after my sister, Kristiana, who died in her infancy.

"I brought K home to the shipping container in order to show my family the good thing I'd found. My mother agreed to let me tie her to a stake in the sand until my father returned. When he did, we stood and watched her as she shyly turned on her rope.

"*You missed something*, my father said, happily. *She's branded. She belongs to someone else. You can't have her.*"

The priest grabbed a long stick from the ground and drew a symbol in the dirt:

"This was the mark," he said, "that had been burned into her body. I was not allowed to keep her. Later that night, after my father let K loose to wander away down the beach, I heard him whisper to my mother: *Day after day, week after week, year after year—his life avoids him.*"

The priest clapped his hands together. "His life avoids him," he repeated.

"I'm sorry," she said. She stared at the mark, which seemed to recede, over and over, into itself. "But the pony wasn't yours."

"One more thing," he said, holding his stick across her path. "Let me finish plain. Let me be honest. After all these years, it is not my pony that I miss. It is not my pony named K, or even Kristiana, my dead sister. I do not miss them. Not at all! It is the mark that I miss. I am waiting for the mark to come again."

He raised his blocking stick, but she pushed past him.

Neftali lay amongst shards and shards of finest blue. He looked like he did when he was asleep: monumental.

"Don't sleep," she said, "Don't be funny."

At the sound of her voice, he sat up. Wither his head? Intact, but rearranged. When he looked at her, she saw that his eyes had switched places.

They finished the day's work in silence. Neftali watched her in a new way and could not regain his balance or make it back up the ladder to the roof. He dug pits for roses and peered at her. She wandered out of his sight to gather stones. He followed and watched from a distance, holding his shovel diagonally across his chest like a sword.

In the weeks after the fall, Neftali began to accuse his sisters and his poor, pale mother of harlotry. And when the priest installed himself in the offices of the glass chapel, burning himself regularly while bathing nude on the pews in the amplified sun, Neftali became unmanageable.

One morning, she hung a red towel on the line, and Neftali jumped out from behind a hedge. "What is this?" he screamed, grabbing the towel. "A signal?"

He wrung the towel and gritted his teeth to keep from crying out but could not, at last, contain himself. "You witch," he said, "I knew you would not last. Why flash your signal where I can see? Why not visit him in secret? You make me witness!"

She did not explain herself, as one would not to a swarm of flies or a storm.

She told her husband that Neftali had lost his way. "It was the fall," she said. "He's not the same." From his bed, her husband dismissed him, and Neftali left at once, with all his sisters and his mother. It was a hot dry day, and she hid inside her house, watching him go.

Her children were playing elsewhere. Her brother-in-law stood on the stone balcony of La Casetta, smoking a cigarette in his torn robe. She motioned for him to go back inside, and he laughed, leaning out over the wide marble railing to expose himself through the great rift in his silken garment. He waved enthusiastically to Neftali, who would not wave back.

Sisters and mother walked away holding baskets and healthy houseplants. Neftali followed, dragging a heavy trunk that left a dark scar on the grass. She could not see her husband, but she could see a growth. It was everywhere, edging out her home, and it showed no sign of stopping. What now? she asked herself and wished to see Neftali turn and drag himself back to her with his old and sweeping gaze.

Later that night, she went down to the garden to listen to the water steps. In the sound of the fall of the water, she heard her own voice and the voices of several interesting men, and she asked:

"Do I want one?"

No, decidedly not.

"Did I ever?"

Not even as a child.

"What is it I'm missing?"

Ritual violence.

"Shouldn't I suffer the same as you?"

For what? We are not alike.

"No?"

No.

"Then tell me: What am I?"

You are lucky. You are free.

Now another voice rose up to drown the others—the roaring of the ocean. It was never far away, and yet she had not come to know it. She scanned the darkness, which was charged with an indescribable loneliness. Elsewhere, a foghorn blew. The sound had no match on earth. For some time after it faded, she thought of herself as happy.

My Last Client

MY VERY LAST CLIENT WAS A REFUGEE BY BIRTH. It had been decades since the great pouring-in but his offness still showed around the eyes, and for this he was mildly persecuted by the people who lived on the snowy island. This persecution was a chill he was always catching. It was nestled in the angle of every native face like a private glacier tended by a miser in the shadow of his counting hut.

When we walked through town together, my client often mentioned that his feet were numb and he didn't know why—he didn't understand that a certain type of sock was being withheld from him. Instead, he saw himself as vital in the way of a variance, and a dedicated consumer to boot. But when I, who by birth belonged, looked at him, I saw a man nearly entombed in social ice, whose only possibility for escape was contained in his left eye, only this single one of his features—like someone's idea of a joke—resembled a native's and gestured toward the possibility of escape.

My client was awfully attractive—fierce of face and black hole staring. But he was also long-chest and weak-necked, and he had a pensioner's taste in clothing. On top of that, he took a too-broad view of his intelligence. There was no topic he would not debate. In particular, he enjoyed lively conversations that seemed to be about natural history but were actually somnambulant rehearsals of the manifesto that had failed his parents (they were coming through, you see, to further set him apart; each conversation he had was in this way corrosive). But in spite of all that, he was almost universally desired, especially by the elderly—plus exchange students, tourists, in-patients, et cetera—so as his support contact, it was my job to help him maintain a manageable pace, which I could do quite well because he was not desired by me.

When I took him through the streets, I behaved as if I had a mad horse on lead. I blinded him against the twinnish teens, which was for his own good, and I whispered soothing stuff when we passed the hair salon. I wasn't against a good time, but it still got me when they came up sidling sly, chill of face but hot of body, asking for a ride. They—who would never sit in his one big room or ask him down from the ridge to share a potato or take him to the hothouse with a shaker of salt— sought his amorous attention with great energy. They—who would never think of loving him—asked like beggars to be plunged by his exotic instrument. They were the mad ones! So, yes, my job sometimes made me desperate about the future of things. Though I did, almost always, once he'd been approached, let him go.

But as soon as we were on the ski trails, far away from the kiosks and the whale-pots flaming high against the ice, I would mentally unbridle him, and we would frolic on the freshly tracked snow and crouch in the under-pine like thieves. This was not part of my job, but I mention it in order to show that

I was not entirely immune to his charms. We rarely spoke, except about the temperature of his feet and sometimes about the possibility of his one-day obtaining skis. Although I knew this would never happen, I enjoyed imagining it with him. I loved the thought of his extra-long middle swooping left beyond the trees and its taking, because of his torso's extraordinary length, at least two blinks more for his head to disappear. But this, as I conceived it, was not an erotic slowing of time. This was purely aesthetic on my part, and maybe a little pitying. I wanted him to go longer, much longer, than the time remaining to him on earth. I wanted his body to begin and end elsewhere, at home, meaning *his* home, wherever that was, meaning even I, whose job was to include him, wanted him out.

When I dropped him off at the end of the day, I'd head straight to the silent movie theater and sit in the front row by myself with one beer and a glass of water and watch the girl at the piano, who seemed to have been carved from the under-ice, whose face was so determined that she could not express. What I've described so far is typical island, but she was not—she was ultra-typical and in that way extraordinary. Plus she was unseeing and completely devoid of life. She played music without playing music. She never—ever—turned to the audience. She was the mold!

After the film, I'd walk home through the streets with a sway in my step. I'd allow myself to parse the pianist until the hangman's cart, then I'd stop and buy a length of candied rope. Then the hangman would say, "How's it hanging," and I'd say, "I have no idea," and we'd both bow our heads and snicker.

After that, I'd take a seat on the highest bench, prop my legs up on the snow, and sum her up. I almost always came to the same conclusion, with periodic variations that I attributed to the length of that day's rope: I could break myself against her. I could vanish into pieces. I could be like a secret crack spreading fast through the ice of her body and not even she would know I was there until it was far too late.

In truth, I had no real plans with regard to women. I intended to take no action. I was a support contact in a medium-sized village, and I was still relatively young. I knew that even the pianist, who seemed the absolute height of chill, could turn out to be one of those who came to my doorstep in tears requesting clarification, or who obscured the existence of the outer-sock from my charge, but still willingly took a turn with him behind my back.

One day I picked him up early—I wanted to hit the shrimp-stand before evening—and he was still in his robe. He asked me inside while he dressed, and I protested—I wasn't supposed to enter his home, it was in violation of my role as representative of the outer-social—but then I spied the flirty tips of two skis peeking out from behind a large jacket hanging in the hallway. I asked him where he'd gotten the skis. He dropped his robe and laced his fingers together around the back of his neck. His penis was sturdy and smooth, his pubic hair sculpted into the shape of the rising sun. There was a flicker in his left eye.

"I went out last night," he said. He stood in the middle of his one big room.

"Without me?"

"Yes. I went to Grunder. Have you been?"

"The club?"

"Yes, the club." He blinked. "What can I say? I wanted connection."

"Did you like it?" I moved the jacket aside. The skis were made of birch. I could tell by the smooth slope of their smile that they'd spent many winters on the snow.

He watched me with the skis, keenly, as if he were their parent. "No, I didn't like it. It was awful. They served me wine in a glass with no stem. A night-child stole my coat. I went outside to catch my breath and my feet froze. Then I staggered around without feeling. My feet were two blocks of ice. I spent one whole hour in the snow. But that's not all that happened."

He sighed and moved to his refrigerator, which was next to his single bed. There was no shower. There was no toilet. There was a pail and a long-handled scoop. He opened the refrigerator door and a cloud enveloped his lower body. He drank greedily from a brown bottle of fish oil. His torso trembled.

"You found your way home in the end," I said. "So, no problem. But next time, let me know when you're in need of company. There's no need for you to go anywhere alone. I'm your friend."

"You're my support contact."

He had never called me that before, and I was surprised to find that it stung. He quickly dressed and pulled some over-socks ceremoniously from a plastic tub beneath his single bed. He pulled them slowly, proudly up over his calves. "I've made some friends," he said, "as you can see."

I saw. He'd made contact of another kind. Of course, this was the goal, but I hadn't guided the connection and so couldn't be sure of its health. I wasn't able to remember what the hand-book prescribed for situations like this, but I found that I didn't really care. I was pleased that someone had seemingly rewarded him for his services for once—and so generously. I smiled. I let my lips hang open. I was tempted to drop my guard entirely, to quit, to propose a different sort of arrangement.

"After that awful hour in the snow," he said, "I passed a church. I was frozen to the heels. The door was open, and there was a lecture going on inside, so I slipped in the back and sat near the heater to thaw. Why haven't you taken me there? It's perfect. A perfect space. There are purple candles that melt into white wax. And it smells good too… like a meat I've never eaten but whose taste I can clearly recall…"

"Are you almost ready?" I asked, feeling tender. "We have lots to do today."

He was prancing around in his socks, stepping high, his left eye flickering faster and faster.

"Almost," he said. He took his old brown boots from atop the radiator and smelled them. Then he fell back on the couch and bent his leg and pulled his boot, with some difficulty, over the over-sock. He sat on the couch with his elbows on his knees and his legs wide apart.

"The lecture," he said, "was about the earth's groaning. It was about the necessity of tuning ourselves in to the frequency of this groaning. Not because the groaning is an indicator of the earth's current pleasure or displeasure, but because it's a forecast—the groaning is the sound of the impending abolition of Family or Future. This was the night's debate. Which one is on its way out? Family or Future? There's a big difference, but the lecturer admitted that even though she's the world's foremost expert on earth groan, she is only *advanced*. She's not fluent. So basically she was saying that she can't do it herself, but needs more people to become advanced in earth groan, which would involve, as a first step, everybody paying closer attention to their surroundings. So that we might be able to converse, gain fluency, and reach a consensus regarding which F-word is at stake. It was billed as a lecture, but it was really more of a call to arms. I found it exhilarating."

He massaged his knees. "But I can't learn a thing," he said. "You, best of all, know my limits. So even though I appreciated her project, I felt free of any duty to respond to her call. I remain free. But anyway, there was a girl in my row. She was with her elderly mother. The girl kept raising her hand and sniffing until the lecturer was forced to call on her. And the girl said her mother was *already fluent* in earth groan and that obviously Family had already been abolished—I mean, look around!— but Future wasn't the right F-word either. Future was not at risk. It was Film. Film would be abolished. The lecturer was not amused. She didn't think the earth would deign to comment on something as insignificant as Film."

"Well, would it?" I was similarly inclined. After all, I was at the movies every day and still had almost no relationship with the screen.

He looked at me. Then he began to move slowly around the room, filling his day bag: a carton of apple juice, his tattered wallet, a sack of nuts. "I'm disappointed in you," he said.

"One of the attitudes of the island," I said, assuming, despite myself, my most professional tone, "is that the earth is no-nonsense. The earth is indifferent to our survival, which is why we love her so much. She isn't concerned with fictions."

"What about documentaries? What about movies about the earth?"

"That sounds like flattery," I said, "which is another thing the earth can't stand."

He stood before his mirror, tapping the skin around his eyes. "In any case," he said, "the old woman was very upset that the lecturer was like you about the earth and Film. I haven't mentioned that the old woman was really, really old. Practically calcified. But perfect. Just perfect in her way. She had a custom seat with wooden wheels. I've never seen anything like it. Also she couldn't really talk except with her fingers, and her agitation showed that way, through her fingers, she flicked them all around, really, really fast, and her daughter translated for the rest of us what she was saying with her hands, and it was something like: She's disappointed in your dearth of imagination. She hates your attitude. She calls it island-provincial. She blames you in advance for the abolition of Film, after which will come the abolition of Fun and the abolition of Fine Food and finally the abolition of Flesh until we are all just a herd of skeletons in over-socks who have no idea how to have a good time."

"Which is how you learned about the over-sock," I said. I went around the room turning off the lights. "Really, we've got a lot to do today," I said, trying to sound cheerful. I encouraged him toward the door.

He went out into the blazing white snow and shaded his eyes. "Well, yes," he said, "but I did not really *know* the over-sock until I held the over-sock in my own two hands, which happened when the girl and her mother took me to their house on the other side of the island. It's near the little beach where I like to swim. We must have passed it a hundred times. They have a room that is all rugs. Made of some dark-furred animal. The kind of rug that is basically a life. And there's a massive fireplace. So big. Just huge."

There, in the snow, he resembled a too-early flower. Beautiful and frail and destined to slump without the aid of some unnatural prop.

He aimed his chin at me. "Don't look at me like that," he said. "Don't question me with your eyes. I'll just tell you, really plain. I plunged them both. And I liked it, with both of them, but more with the old woman. A lot more. Like I might be in love. And for the first time in my life, I was offered juice afterward, and conversation, and over-socks, and skis, and I'm upset, I am, that you never offered this to me, not even as a possibility. You never told me I could get this far with anyone."

He was angry with me, giving free rein to his disappointment, and it felt unexpectedly awful. But I had not done anything wrong. I had not offered him this possibility because I had not believed in it. I still didn't. Moving forward, he would need all the protection I could offer.

"My job is not to predict the future," I said. "My function is support."

I lingered in the hallway. I gently fingered the tip of the skis. "The socks are fine," I said. "You can keep them. But the skis are too advanced. We'll have to take them back."

The flicker in his eye sped up, then slowed to black. "Whatever," he said and walked toward the bus stop.

I heaved the skis over my shoulder and followed with my heart on silent. I let myself inhabit the mute and immediate future of that evening, when I would be alone in the velvet row with my double glass, free to fail to listen to the music she was not playing. Free to see nothing of the screen. Free to slide my stare down her frozen profile and plummet off the tip of her nose.

Despite the excitement of the night before, my client wanted his usual shopping. We stopped at the international grocery for his bit of dried pork and currants. The dandy in the bookstore had taken the liberty of ordering a few books he thought my client might like. I flipped through them at the counter while my client browsed the back shelves pouting. They were sweet little reads without moral or adventure, haphazardly peppered with sex. I could see what the dandy was after, and usually I would have let it go, but when citing the excuse of his extraordinary neatness, he asked my client to remove his shoes and socks before coming through the curtain into the back and to please refrain from touching any of the hung icons and to think about taking as few deep breaths as possible in order to avoid tainting the sheets, I called the whole thing off. "He's exhausted," I said to the dandy. "You would be too."

My client was unfazed by the blip in our routine. It was clear he had other things on his mind. He passed the bakery where he'd spent many afternoons plunging two hypothermic sisters without giving it a second glance. He explained, as we walked, that he could last longer with his new over-socks. He did not feel compelled to enter the shops in order to warm up, in fact, he felt free—freer than he'd ever felt before—and so talkative! By the statue of the famous harpoonist, he embraced me. I stared at the flayed tip of the deadly tool and let my chin sink into his chest. A gull tried to land there but couldn't. The skis lay in the snow where they'd fallen at the moment of his descent upon me.

"I'm not lonely," he said, "but that's the problem. I feel like I haven't been taken seriously. I haven't been given a chance."

"That might be true," I said, grabbing the skis and assuming a business-like attitude, although, this, too, had hurt me— that in surveying his social history, he had not seen me. I had not appeared. So what was I doing here?

"The trails?" he said, brightening. "Please—the trails. Can we go? It'll make me feel better."

"Sure," I said, determined to lighten the mood. "Why not?" They were still unmarked, which was unusual this late into the morning and which I felt boded well for our fun. I stowed the skis in the under-pine and we hopped along like bunnies. I blasted him in the face with a ball of snow, and a little blood showed on his lip but he didn't care. We laughed. I fell onto the knobby root of a tree that was hidden by a drift and it landed like a knee in the middle of my back. I crowed in pain and we laughed at that too. We stopped laughing when he sat down by the skis and touched them and looked at me, his desire painfully plain.

"I don't know how to put them on," he said.

It was hard to say—but I had to say it. "You know I can't let you."

He took a ski and threw it like an athlete. It glided soundlessly into the trees, down the side of the ridge, toward the ocean and out of sight.

We stood side-by-side and looked at the water. It was beautiful, crinkled and blue.

"Do you think I broke it?" he said.

"No, it was well-made. It was old. It had been taken good care of for a very long time by someone who loved it a lot. But we'll never find it now. No matter. We'll still have to return the one."

The house was just as he'd described. It was very near the little beach, so near that it was practically on the shore, but it was firmly hidden from sight by a dense stand of trees. It was single-story and made of whole logs whose branches had not been removed so that the place had the feeling of a spontaneous architecture. The ocean was audible but otherwise unreal. At the door, my client adjusted his hair before ringing the bell. When I heard light footsteps approaching, I threw the single ski out of sight along the edge of the house. He looked at me in surprise but said nothing.

The girl didn't ask who-who through the thick wooden door, but flung it open and turned on her heels. "Come in," she said. "I'll be right back."

Her face was visible for only a moment but I would have recognized her at the bottom of a well—it was the pianist. I turned away, momentarily overwhelmed by her many movements. My client stepped inside like he owned the place.

"Sigi," he called. "I'm back!"

I followed him inside, my head down. He led me through a mix of hallways to a large room filled with dark-furred rugs, the fluffiest near the fire. He took off his boots and over-socks and even his socks, and stretched out on the fluff, spreading his toes. He looked at me pityingly. "Sit down," he said. "Take it easy."

I wanted to. I wanted to stretch out beside him and make a joke or two about the lives gone flat beneath us, but I couldn't.

Only once had I ever seen the pianist break face. The film was not over but was coming to an end, I could tell by the pace of her fingers on the keys, when a terrible flapping noise arose. The film had broken, the screen went white. I glanced at it for the first time—it was like a field of snow. The theater and everyone in it was suddenly lit up. Every face was a moon, and we could not stop rubbing our eyes, we could not stop turning around to peek at each other like children. But she didn't stop playing. And she didn't look, not at us, and not at the screen. I thought I saw a sudden shift in the topography of her profile, a gathering of flesh around her chin, a sudden jerk at the corner of her mouth as if she had been hooked by someone floating far above. But it was over in an instant. She was back to ice, and I could not be sure of what I'd seen.

The girl wheeled her mother through the doorway, stopping at the edge of the rugs. Her face, here in her home, was animated, her expressions spastic—I was pained by her lively aspect.

Her mother, however, was permanent in that reassuring way. Her eyes hung back in their stony sockets, her mouth was iron hard. Her nose was bound to itself and her breath had no effect. I was determined to look only at her.

"Help me with Sigi," said the girl. My client hopped to his feet, and I turned away to catch my breath.

There were the sounds of work, of the rearranging of things.

"There," said my client tenderly. "You're with me by the fire, Sigi."

He laughed, and the girl laughed, but there was no way to tell if Sigi was laughing or not.

"She's saying how glad she is to see you again," said the girl. "She's been thinking about you since you left."

"And I've been thinking of you, Sigi," he said. "And of what you gave me. Tell her that."

"Now she's telling you that it was nothing. She's asking you not to thank her. Act like a wolf, not a colleague, she says. The earth prefers it."

"But what do you prefer, Sigi?" said my client. I knew that tone well. He was flirting.

I examined the wall of logs. I tried to take myself to the under-pine, far away from the warm and fluffy room. I was fleeing to the place of our togetherness—I just wanted to be with my friend! Then I heard a shifting, a sliding around, which recalled me to the room. There was a creeping quiet. When I could no longer stand not to know, I looked. Sigi had been undressed. The girl was folding her mother's clothing, using the older woman's body as a surface for that folding, and my client was removing his pants.

"Are we sure?" I said, holding my own hand. "Is everyone absolutely sure that this is what we want to do?"

Unclothed, Sigi was the color of driftwood. Her neck arced sharply so that her head could not lie flat. She was staring upside down at the wall behind her, her crown bearing maximum weight. Her legs had dropped to the side—they were hooked and tangled together—but the rest of her torso lay flat. Her breasts seemed to have been cured. They clung like scabs to the rack of her ribs. My client kneeled down beside her.

"Wait," I said. "Everyone wait."

The girl came to stand beside me. She leaned against the wall. I would not look at her. I couldn't. So I would have to look at Sigi. At my client. At what they were about to do together. I had never watched a plunging before.

"Sigi likes him," said the girl. "And I don't feel a drop of jealousy."

"But, can she?" I said. "And what will it mean? I mean, is she?"

"Is she what?" said the girl. "Alive?"

Sigi's fingers began to flick. Faster and faster around the petrified core of her body as if she were a tree bewitched.

"She says not to watch if it upsets you to see an old woman enjoying herself," said the girl. "She says there is always the door. She asks you to do what you want, but she also asserts that the earth will no longer stand to have its human needs ignored."

My client began to plunge. The sounds of Sigi's pleasure drifted softly from the hole of her mouth.

"It's a sight to see," said the girl. "Fun is the only thing I have eyes for anymore. I can't even watch a film, which upsets my mother. The real truth is"—she began to whisper—"I don't think Film can be saved. Things have gone too far. And I can't bear to watch a thing I love marching forward as if nothing will ever change, oblivious to the fact of its impending destruction!"

The girl slipped her arm through mine, but I would not lean into the gesture. "Does the earth still speak to you?" she asked. "Do you hear what the groaning says?"

"I don't know."

"You should listen. It's giving its very last lessons."

"And then what?" I said.

"Then nothing! Let's go have some juice."

But I didn't want juice. I wanted him. But by this one preposterous act he had outgrown me.

I got down on all fours and crawled across the soft expanse. The body of my client and the body of the old woman were a bridge that spanned the ages. He rose from her like a thing from its fossil. Then he sank back down into her body, which was his custom-fitted grave. The top of his head moved up and down, up and down as he plunged, while she hardly moved at all.

I got close. Closer. Face-to-face with the top of his head and her upside-down eyes. I peered into Sigi's black, windless depths and found myself reflected there. I was still young but my mouth—my mouth was not. I groaned.

And as if I'd jerked his lead, my client looked up at me. He paused in his plunging and was still. His right eye softened with warmth for me. But his left eye was flickering fast. I took a good long look and saw that something was moving there, inside of his eye—it was a film. I sat back to watch, my butt nestled cozily in a sea of fluffy rugs. The film came into focus, framed by the leggy length of his lashes. It showed my client, up on the ridge of the island. There he was, alone on the unmarked trails, his back to the camera, skiing. His moves were expert. He swished side-to-side, so sexy and so sure. Then he swooped left behind the trees, his extra-long torso taking its time, and disappeared.

The Wallet

I WAS GETTING OFF THE BUS WHEN A MAN STOPPED ME to ask if I'd lost my wallet. He'd found one on the seat I'd just vacated and was now offering it to me. The wallet was smooth and pale like something private that had been bared without its owner's consent. I told the man no, the wallet wasn't mine, it couldn't be, I didn't own one. He looked at me, unblinking, and said nothing more.

When I arrived at my office, I saw that the small exterior pocket of my green backpack, the one that would have held a wallet if I had owned one, was unzipped and hanging open. This was the part of my backpack that would have been visible to the man as I went before him down the aisle. He must have felt certain that the wallet was mine, given both the state of my pocket and the fact that he'd found it on my seat, which would account for his confusion. I decided then that his expression had not communicated disappointment, as I'd assumed, but something more primitive, like fear.

As I thought about the man and his impression of me, I began to wonder if it was true that I didn't own a wallet. It seemed possible that I might, at some point, have purchased one. It was an object that people did tend to own, and I was a person who tended to do what others did, with just a few meaningful exceptions. But if I had, at some point, purchased a wallet, would I have purchased that particular one?

I tried to access my own tastes, but they eluded me. And because I did not know what I liked, I could not be sure whether such a wallet would have appealed to me at the point of purchase. I searched the pocket of my backpack for a sign—a coin, a photograph of a child, a laminated prayer—anything that a wallet might have contained, but I seemed to have left the house with just a small square mirror, an empty vial, and a library book. The pockets of my jacket were empty.

A person did need money to survive. It was an essential accessory, and I was a living, breathing person so far as I could tell. Though I felt strongly that I was not someone who needed things, I *was* sitting in my place of work, which meant I did have a job, which meant that I must have or have had money, and, having had money, I would have needed a place to keep it, so at some point, it did seem to follow, I would have owned a wallet. I couldn't think of my wallet, past or present, but that did not mean it didn't exist. And because I had been told, recently, by a slim young psychologist I'd met at a three-day party, that the simplest explanation was almost always the correct one, I concluded that the wallet on the bus must have been mine. The man had been right, after all, to fear me.

I looked around my office. I had closed the door. On the back of it, someone had hung a poster depicting the phases of the moon. But who? Who liked the moon? Not me, not *I*, who had most definitely been on the bus, of that I was sure, but, if it was true that I had no money, why had I been allowed to board?

I tried to remember the face of the bus driver but couldn't. Had I said something to him to gain access? Or had I walked right by? Had I seemed to be refusing to pay? And had I earned, by that refusal, some sort of protected status? Was I allowed, now, to do exactly as I pleased? And, if so, what would I do next?

At my desk, before the dark computer, I shivered with pleasure. It was so easy to encounter someone who was out of touch, who was not entirely *with it*. It could happen anywhere, even on the bus.

On my way to the office bathroom, I ran into a colleague. She had just returned from a vacation to an island where there were many monasteries, mostly inactive.

"I'm going to need your help this week," she said. "I was injured on vacation, and I can't lift anything over ten pounds. I have to move some reports. Boxes of them. Very heavy."

"Sure," I said.

"Boxes and boxes of very important reports describing the very important plans of people who are no longer relevant. They're headed straight to the dumpster," she said, tapping her forehead.

She was standing in the middle of the hallway with her right leg thrust forward. Her long skirt was hiked up and tucked tenuously under the elastic of her loose beige underwear, revealing her bandaged thigh. Above the bandage, a section of her way upper leg was showing.

I looked at the exposed rectangle of skin and wondered if what I was looking at was in fact obscene. "What happened to your leg?"

She looked pityingly at herself but made no adjustments to her skirt. She seemed entirely comfortable baring that high privacy. "Vacation didn't go like I thought. But it never does, does it?"

I recalled my last vacation during which I'd traveled alone to a coastal city. A few days in, I'd seen a child's head squeezed unto death by the gates of an underground metro. I remembered the child's face—mask-like—and the color of the mother's skin—lunar. Vacation, as far as I knew, was not something you thought about in advance of its happening. It was more like a surprise assault. "You didn't enjoy yourself?"

"I'm glad you asked," she said. "I did enjoy myself, in a way. I'd planned to visit all the monasteries, but the island turned out to be a much bigger place than the internet had suggested. There was actually just one monastery within walking distance of my hotel. It was straight uphill from town, visible from the rooftop, and it still took me two-and-a-half hours to get there. The first two times I made the trip, the gates were closed, and nobody answered the bell. The third time, I brought an LP by my favorite singer, the one I've so far made sure not to tell anyone about, the epinoiac who lost all that weight. She just pretended that she'd already eaten. That's all you have to do these days. Nobody cares if you waste away. Nobody acknowledges a disappearance, so long as you keep it public.

"Anyway, on my third visit, the gate was closed like before, but this time there was a pile of spiralized orange peels on the ground outside, so I knew someone must be inside. I walked all the way around the building, sticking close to the exterior wall. Sometimes I thought I could hear laughing coming from inside. Not the laughing of a person. Just laughing."

She itched herself along the edge of her bandage. The skin, wherever she touched it, turned red and rose slightly. "When I'd gone all the way around and arrived back at the front of the monastery, the gate was open."

Up and down the office hallway, doors began to close. I leaned against the wall and closed my eyes. "Oh yeah?"

She lowered her voice. "I don't know if you've ever stood at the entrance to a monastery, but I can tell you that it is not a comfortable feeling. It's like: Do you even want to know?

Like, do you even want to *think* about what's inside? But I was there, and I was definitely thinking about it. There was no turning back. I'd walked for hours to get there, and my knees ached. In a way, I felt like I deserved it. I was on vacation. Plus, I'd brought a gift for the monks. An album that was secretly spiritual, just like me.

"I stood on the threshold forever, like for the length of this conversation we're having, just staring inside. There wasn't much there. A sunny courtyard of white stone, with a little chapel in the middle. The chapel had no windows. It didn't seem to have a door either. No laughing, not that I could hear. Not anymore. A great loneliness overwhelmed me. I thought of a child I'd never met, a child who had died but failed to realize it and so had gone on living. How I hated that child! How I wished he'd never been born! And then a mule appeared in the courtyard. It clomped slowly out from behind the chapel, wearing a beautiful, beaded harness, its reins dragging on the ground. In its mouth, it held an orange, which by some magic—its lips—was slowly spinning. Its lips were moving the orange, and the peel was being removed, in an intact spiral, by the mule's teeth. It was delicate work, requiring a patience I hadn't known animals could have. Which is when I realized that the mule was not an animal. It was infertile, like God is. Like God has become."

Here she paused for effect, but before the effect could take hold—I was, by nature, on a delay—she went on.

"Then I had a vision," she said. "It was of myself. I was in the courtyard, and I was a man. I could tell I was a man because I didn't marvel anymore. I didn't wonder. I just circled the mule, wearing a pair of white jeans in the style of a decade during which I'd not been alive. They were much too big for me, the jeans, so I'd cinched them tight with the rope that my older brother had used to hang himself. To an outsider, I might have seemed to be assessing the mule, or maybe coveting its harness. But I wasn't. I was just looking. I didn't even care. At that distance from wonder, I was truly alive. After I'd circled the mule three or four times, I stopped directly behind it. The mule's tale swished. The orange peel dropped whole onto the courtyard floor, and just then I extended my hand and patted the mule's butt.

"In that moment, I was so close to myself, spiritually— you can't imagine, being two-in-one. The distance between us collapsed, and the mule kicked us in the groin. We were very badly injured, maybe permanently. What if we had been crushed? Perhaps, I thought, if I could see it, our penis, I would know more. So, I straddled me. I untied the familiar rope. I unbuttoned our pants. I was hairless, just like my brother was before he died. And then I saw it."

My colleague paused. With her hands, she framed the exposed skin of her leg. Her eyes flashed with unreasonable excitement.

"It's not what you're thinking," she said. "The penis wasn't the thing. What I saw was the thigh of God. I was not supposed to see it—God had not consented. But I saw the thigh of God as the man in me died. And it was no surprise. In fact, I'd seen it many times before—because it was my own."

She stood there, regarding me loosely. I could have been any-one. But I still felt that something was required by the situation.

"On my way out," she said, "I heard the epinoiac's singing. The monks had got their hands on the record, probably while I was visioning. It was a theft, when you think about it. By the monks. I didn't give it to them, even though I'd intended to. But I don't blame them. You have to steal experience. That's what I've learned. It's the only way to get it."

"Wow," I said. I wasn't against the story, or theft, but I did have to pee, so I tried to wrap things up. "You know I'm here if you need help. All you have to do is ask. I can lift whatever."

"I know that," she said, her out-thrust leg making it difficult for me to pass. "You're always very helpful. But it's still nice to hear, from someone, that they are who you think they are."

In the bathroom, I didn't wipe. I didn't have the patience, or maybe it was care I didn't have for myself or the things I owned. On the way back down the hallway, I popped my head into my colleague's office.

"By the way," I said. "I've lost my wallet. If you see it, let me know."

She was sitting awkwardly at her desk, her leg stiff and extended, staring at a map on her computer screen. A bright blue dot was moving slowly across the screen, along the curving line that depicted a road.

"How awful," she said, her eyes glassy. "Did you know you can watch the progress of the bus now? In real time?" She tracked the bright blue dot with her finger, leaving an oily smear on the screen.

"Well, you can," she said. "I don't know what this is supposed to add to my life. The bus isn't more of a bus if I know where it is when it's not with me. In fact, in a way, it's less of one. You should never know where the bus is. You should never know when, exactly, the bus is going to arrive. Don't you agree? It has so far been in the nature of a bus to arrive around the time you expect it to, but it's important to preserve the possibility of its never coming. The bus should not be a given. It should feel, every time, like the miraculous return of something useful—even necessary—that you'd worried might be gone for good."

A Common
Scene

I WAS STANDING AT MY WINDOW READING A LONG FAX from Marie when a stranger began to call up to me from the street.

The fax concerned a fundraiser held to support the construction of a zoological garden—an event at which Marie and I had both been present. Something had happened to her there, something she hoped I might be able to confirm, but what that something was, she had not yet disclosed despite the fact that I'd been reading the fax for ten minutes. By the time the stranger called up, the length of Marie's prefatory framing had begun to bother me, and I felt a growing resistance to confirming her version of events, whatever it might be.

Despite my reluctance to read on, I did my best to appear engrossed in the document, not wanting to engage with the stranger who could not have been calling up to anyone else—as far as I knew, I was the only one in my building who rose before 6 a.m. The other occupants were outpatients of a nearby hospital who suffered from an unresearched illness the primary symptom of which was a rarefied fatigue. Unlike many people, I believed this illness was real, which was why I'd been allowed to take up residence in the building though I was not, myself, a sufferer.

The fundraiser had not been held at the site of the zoological garden—though that would have been nice, and more convincing—out of sensitivity to those of the donors' guests who might have found the establishment of such a facility to be out of touch with current sensibilities or perhaps even offensive, but this could not have been what concerned Marie, who took offense to just one category of thing, which was medical gaslighting. The fundraiser had instead been held at the large and somewhat ostentatious estate of the garden's primary donor, Mr. Gray Turpin, who had not allowed his guests to roam freely through his house but had confined us to a smallish ballroom that opened onto a reflective pool bound on all sides by a tall hedge.

Again, the stranger called up. I'd been careful not to look at him directly, and I refused to do so now, though I could see in my peripheral vision that he'd begun to wave his arms. It occurred to me that he might be able to sense that I was not truly focused on the activity of reading the fax, so I committed to it in earnest.

All of this is to say that I know how difficult I can be, and I'm grateful to you for so quietly receiving the several bombs I've lobbed at you recently—you are so like a friend. Now I need to toss one more your way: I am disturbed by an encounter I had at the fundraiser with a young man named Nicholas.

At least that's the name he gave me. We were monopolizing a bowl of olives, plunging our fingers in to force an intimacy, which, as you know, is my practice when eating in groups, and he used this similarity between us as his opening, though he turned shortly after to the subject of my glasses.

Did you notice the glasses I was wearing at the fundraiser? Do you remember where I got them? I found them on our trip to the desert all those many years ago. They were lying at the base of that massive boulder. The lenses were cracked. I only recently got around to having them refitted with my prescription. I know you and I no longer speak, but I have to say: it hurts that you didn't notice them, or that if you did, you didn't indicate that you had, didn't send me any sign, however subtle (can't we sometimes bend the rules?). I always thought we had a very nice time in the desert, despite how poorly you were sleeping. Who knows how you're sleeping now.

I'd always disliked Marie's habit of imbuing minor events with special importance, like the discovery of these glasses, which I did not remember at all, not in the slightest, though I was able to recall many other frightening scenes from that very trip in great detail.

"Hey!" the stranger called.

It was outrageous that he was still there. Unbelievable, even. Perhaps he was sick.

I held the fax even closer to my face.

Anyway, I'm not sure what gave this young man the courage—there were at least twenty years between us—but he boldly announced that I did not need my glasses, that I was in fact wounding myself by wearing them. He went on to describe the method by which he'd cured his own myopia, which amounted to a long campaign of staring at distant objects. He'd had a dream, he said, in which it had been revealed to him that his glasses were a weakening device, given to him by his parents, in order to extend his dependence on their charity.

By this time, I'd noticed a fresh set of stitches along his hairline, four wiry knots crusted with blood. I felt queasy and asked if he wanted to get some water—we had, between the two of us, polished off the olives—and he agreed. As we walked toward the refreshment table, I tried to catch the eye of any other guest—you were nowhere in sight— but there was something about our pairing that repulsed observation. Though I am generally quite intruded upon, I was given absolute privacy as I moved through the crowd with this strange person, so much so that I wondered if I had become, to the rest, invisible.

The thought sent me into a panic—you know how important it is to me to be seen. I needed air, I looked around for an exit. In a display of extraordinary sensitivity to my needs, Nicholas led me swiftly through the French doors to the edge of the reflecting pool, where we stood together in silence as my lenses darkened against the sun. I'd chosen that kind, you see. The lenses were capable of transition.

"Heeeeey. Helloooo," called the stranger.

I was beginning to worry that he might wake the other residents, whose sleep, because of the nature of their illness, was not restorative, meaning it had to be long—over ten hours—to have any effect. If their rest were compromised, I might be blamed, and if I were blamed, I might be evicted. I shivered performatively, then closed the window against the cold that was not there. I did not move out of the stranger's sight, however, as I was hoping to extend the fantasy that I had not noticed him at all. I kept reading.

Once outside, I began to feel a bit better—the reflecting pool was having its effect—though Nicholas seemed to be building himself up to something. I could see his reflection in the water, the fine young figure of him, and it crossed my mind that he might want something erotic to occur. I surprised myself by feeling open to it. It would not be so long, I reminded myself, before I would be that old woman at the base of the boulder. Do you remember her? You must. Who could forget!

The sun was reflected in the pool. It was a bright, loose circle— quite seductive to the eye. I remember that I was about to indicate, energetically, that I was sexually attainable when Nicholas tore my glasses from my face and threw them into the water.

I didn't make a move. I knew not to, from female experience. Instead, I let him hiss his little plan into my ear. Now that he had freed me from charity, he would ask me to open my eyes. He would ask me to watch, as his mother would never, what he would do next. In full possession of his power, clear-sighted and without fear, he would do what every living child had been told they must never do.

I knew better than to stop him. He had already proven that he was unpredictable. Destructive. If he would damage himself, there was nothing I could do.

And then he did it. He stared at the sun.

To steady myself, I watched the pale reflection, extra loose without my glasses, in the reflecting pool.

My own eyes burned with pain referred.

Sorrow. I felt it. I feel it all, as you well know.

After several long minutes, he cried out in exultation. Then he took off toward the hedge, crashing straight through to the other side.

When I was certain he would not return, I went in to find Mr. Turpin. I told him what had happened. He expressed an appropriate amount of shock, though I could see he did not entirely believe me.

His name was Nicholas, I said. He was probably about 20.

Mr. Turpin shook his head.

He had stitches, I said, touching the spot, on my own head, where his stitches had been. And now he's done something very foolish, something that will likely require additional medical attention.

But Mr. Turpin only said, Hm!

Gray, I said soberly. Who was he?

But Mr. Gray Turpin would not play ball. He apologized, he said, but he was not sure if he knew this young man—Nick, was it? There were dozens of donors, and they'd all been allowed one guest. He could not vouch for the character of those who had not themselves donated to the zoological garden, but he was sorry if I'd had a negative experience. He could say, however, that he was an attentive host, and he would certainly have noticed the presence of anyone young at the fundraiser. The garden was not a fashionable cause, these days. He would be surprised if anyone under 30 had risked appearing to support it, by attending.

I dropped the hand that held the long fax from Marie and stared blankly into the middle distance. What exactly did she need from me? She had always been this way, always doubted my interest in her point of view, so she'd found little ways to coerce it, spinning meaningless events into situations urgently requiring my attention. But she could never get to the point too quickly or I might see what was actually there, which was nothing.

As I wondered about the friendship and its ongoing utility to me, I became aware, once more, of the now-muted cries of the stranger, making their way unevenly through the window-pane like the bleating of a freshly slaughtered lamb through the catch of its own blood.

Resentfully, I returned to the fax.

In that case, I told Mr. Turpin, I would need to see the guest list. He balked, but I reminded him of the size of my donation, and he said his secretary would be in touch. In the meantime, he hoped I might be able to recover my experience at the fundraiser by focusing on something else, something he and I could both celebrate, which was what the event showed: There was still a place for the zoological garden in the modern imagination.

Of course, focus was exactly what I could not, anymore, do, so I began to canvass the other guests. I approached them, one by one. Had they brought with them, or had they seen, a young man named Nicholas? They responded conscientiously to my questions, as donors do, but not one would admit to his presence.

As the final round of canapés began to circulate, I was visited by a sudden and terrible desire to lie down. I made my way to the only seating, the padded bench in the entryway, and stretched myself across it. On the opposite wall was the large architectural rendering of the zoological garden. As I stared at the blurry plan, I suddenly recalled having seen you—the back of you—conversing, in that very spot, with a young and healthy head of hair. I remember thinking it strange that you, who never cared for schematics, might be interested in the rendering, and stranger still that you might consent to meeting someone new. I didn't interrupt, of course. I did not indicate, either through sound or movement, that I saw you at all—I've followed your rule, to the letter, ever since the desert.

Now I think you'll agree—I've behaved so well—that I deserve my just reward. Tell me: Was it him? Can you confirm the presence of Nicholas? Weren't your two heads tilted toward each other in a pose suggesting some degree of intimacy (certainly more than you've ever had with me)? If you'll only say that he was present, I promise to drop the matter. I will not go after him for the cost of my glasses—I'm sure he's suffering enough. I only want to know that he was there.

As I contemplated the veracity of Marie's claim that I had a rule, as well as her unpleasant inclusion of the phrase *since the desert*, the fax machine began signaling the arrival of additional pages.

The sun rose into the space between two buildings. A ray of light slashed across my face, as if a great boulder were being moved from the mouth of a cave.

The stranger, inflamed by my glowing visage, renewed his efforts.

"Excuse me!" he cried.

I could hear him clearly now from beyond the pane. He was really getting very loud. I had done my best to vanquish him with neglect, but he was the kind who would have to be dealt with directly.

I raised the window and set my elbows on the sill. The man smiled slightly, crossed his arms, and waited for me to speak. He looked smart and somewhat insane, a new version of that same old character whom I'd not yet had the courage to confront.

I pressed my finger to my lips to buy myself some time. He was bouncing around on the toes of his all-black sneakers. I thought of the sufferers in the building, snug in their single beds, sleeping the sleep of the disbelieved, and it seemed to me that I might be joining them soon if I were not careful.

"People are sleeping," I called down, doing my best to sound apologetic.

"I know you," said the stranger. "You're him."

At the edge of my vision, a delicate band of blue sky began to appear.

"The people who live in this building aren't well," I said. "They need their sleep."

The fax machine was really moving now, knocking and purring and thrusting pages out, so that I struggled, at first, to hear what he said next.

"It *is* you," he said. "I'm sure of it."

Why him? I thought. Not that I expected anything else. When I was younger, I'd assumed I would be compensated, one day, for all the care I'd not received. Someone would come, I thought, someone who would offer me the total experience, and I would finally be free to make a start. But this had not happened. The world was still a dark purse, with strange actors always leaping from its depths.

"I know it's you," he said, this time a little louder. "I saw you there."

I waved my hand around in front of me, as if by doing so I might erase him from the scene.

"I can't do this," I called down to him forcefully. "I'm sorry."

I straightened up, put my hands atop the window like I would close it. He gave me the chance to do so, and when I didn't, he continued.

"I saw you do it," he said, miming a push with his two hands.

A great swell of love for the world overtook me, destroying everything in its path. I looked down upon the stranger with frightful energy, and he glanced up and down the street, trying to bolster himself with the sight of someone else.

But the street was empty. No one was coming. It was just us two on that quiet, almost private, almost deserted, block, and I wondered if perhaps he might think it wise to give it up.

"I saw you in the desert," he said.

A warm breeze carried the smell of dried grass and other natural leavings through the window. I recalled my participation in any number of brutal scenes for which I'd been absolved, most recently by my donation to the zoological garden.

"Wait there," I said.

The stranger's shoulders dropped, and he gave me a ridiculous thumbs up. I closed the window between us and glanced reflexively at the line that was just emerging from the fax machine: *That fundraiser may have been my last. So many times, I have been wounded by my own charity…*

As I looked around for my keys, I cursed myself for reading even a single word more, for once again doing what I'd firmly resolved not to do. After this, I told myself on the stairs, I would change my life. I would close for business, get rid of the fax machine. I would expect less, or nothing, or no one. All roads in, I would destroy.

The door to the street was stuck, as usual. I pressed against it carefully, doling out the weight of my body bit by bit, so that I would not burst forth with any eagerness. The stranger was waiting, his eyes trained nervously on the door that I now came through.

I kept my head down and crossed the street. Without looking at him, I began to walk, and he fell in beside me. My pace was variable in accordance with my patience, and he matched me, stride for stride.

At the intersection, I caught sight of him in the window of an abandoned laundromat. Next to my slumped, reluctant form, he stood tall and young and vigorous. The signal changed, and I charged ahead, turning abruptly into an empty donut shop.

A thin electronic tone announced our entrance. I told the stranger to sit and went alone to the counter. The old woman, her skin thin as pressed flowers, emerged from the back. A grain of regret lodged itself in my throat. Seeing that I was not alone this time, she set two glistening donuts on a paper-lined tray and accepted my payment in the yellowed cup of her hands.

I joined the stranger at a small metal table near the window. He'd chosen the superior seat so that I was forced to look out on the bad-taste cathedral. The road glistened against me and against the others now risen, who dragged themselves hang-necked through the early morning.

I was not one of them. I had been up for hours and beaten them all to the hypnotic void of day. Buoyed by the thought, I watched the stranger take his first bite of the donut for which he had not thanked me. He chewed quickly, numb to the many flakes of glaze that clung to his chin, and I could see that he felt himself to be in the superior position, so casual was his eating.

His other hand lay open on the table, curling naturally around the air, without suspicion, so I slipped mine into it. He stiffened but did not withdraw. I caressed his palm with my finger, and he held my gaze with difficulty.

"You say you saw me," I said. "But how can you be sure?"

"I know it was you," he said, his eyes big and alert.

"But the desert is a common scene."

Now he tried to remove his hand from mine, but I wouldn't let him.

"It *was* you," he said. "I'm sorry. It just was. I was there."

"Is that a fact?" I said bitterly.

"I was there," he said matter-of-factly, "in the desert. On top of the boulder. I was a child, but I remember."

"It could have been anyone," I said, my heart pounding. "You were a child. You didn't know."

The stranger put the donut down. He wiped the glaze from his chin with the back of his free arm. "Listen," he said. "I don't want to make any trouble for you. I'm sure you're mostly a good person. But I saw what you did, and I wonder what it might be worth to you, if I were to promise, you know, that I wouldn't tell anyone else."

Having said it, he hung his head in shame. I felt myself increase in power.

I cast his hand roughly aside and crossed my arms.

"My god," I said. "The arrogance."

"I know you probably aren't like that in real life, but I know what I saw."

"When will you get it through your head?" I snarled. "When will you finally acknowledge your limits? You're sick, do you know that? You need help. When will somebody finally help you?"

"I'm just really low on cash," he said, shifting in his seat so that he could look out onto the street.

"You didn't see me in the desert," I said, leaning forward over the table. "Just as you are not seeing me now."

Then I pinched him, cutting into the soft white underside of his arm with my unkempt fingernails. He winced, then rubbed his arm, hurt.

"You have never seen me," I said. "Never in your life. And that's that."

"That's right," he said as if recalling some lamentable truth. A tear was slowly forming in the corner of his eye, and I longed to see myself in its brimming surface, glowing and golden in the sun that was now streaming through the window.

"There," I said. "That's better. Light is sweet. Not like they told us when we were children. You can look right at it, if you want."

I stared directly at the sun. Mercifully, there was silence in that view. No one to push aside, nothing in the way. The human center was empty.

"Please stop," said the stranger. "I'll go."

"It doesn't hurt."

"Look," he said, "I'm going. I'm leaving now."

"Good," I said, my eyelids fluttering shut despite myself. "And never speak to me again."

"Yes," he said. "Fine."

The thin electronic tone sounded faintly at his exit. I opened my eyes. His silhouette, out on the street, was spangled with yellow spots, his face in deep shadow. He hesitated for a moment then took off down the street at a fast clip.

For a minute or two, I stayed put, watching the yellow spots fade into the gray tabletop. I ate my donut, chewing it thoroughly. The sun warmed the side of my face as I crumpled the napkins, piling them thoughtfully on the stranger's empty tray. It had gone well, all things considered. At least we'd reached an understanding. I was on the verge of throwing myself at my own feet when I remembered that I had not given him my fax number.

I stood abruptly, and a slurry of donut surged up through my throat. The false sun dazzled, bouncing wildly off the display case. Through that obscuring light, I lurched toward the exit and found the old woman standing in it, her features set with the intention to dementedly obstruct.

"Always in my way," I said, putting my hands gently enough on her insubstantial shoulders.

She fell to the floor. I stared with wordless anger as she lay there, open-eyed, in silence. Her glasses lay on the floor next to her, their lenses cracked.

I stepped over her body and burst onto the street.

It wasn't the repetition that hurt. It was the bad taste—now so familiar to me—of that reenactment. Still, I did my part, running half-speed through the steaming streets, the din and the dust of the city kicking up.

I knew the route well, better than he did, so I caught up to him near the quay. Beneath the swaying hook of an unmanned crane, he stood unsuspecting in the company of two young men, talking excitedly. Was he breaking the rules so soon?

The thought enraged me, but I didn't let it show. I wanted my approach to be uncomplicated, but one of the men pointed a finger at me. The stranger saw, blanched, and turned on the heels of his black sneakers, taking off in an unscripted direction.

I gave chase, excited at last. He turned down an alley. I followed, watching him run through traffic and turn the corner at a shuttered bank.

Now my whole effort was to find him. I had been given the power to break loose, to avoid the normal chain of events, and I would not waste it, not this time.

Over the low and ragged rooftop of the metallurgical museum toward which I was now running, the sky wore a rosy collar. The stranger was nowhere in sight, but a sense of my orientation shimmered before me. I recalled the fundraiser, the architectural rendering on the wall, and the young man muttering beside me—*Yes, okay, I was wrong, it wasn't you*—and realized I was one street over from the site of the zoological garden.

I cut through the dark museum. The space was unattended except for the clear plastic donation box. On all sides, the samples glowered from their illuminated recesses. I saw how like them I really was, and it stung. I emerged on the opposite side of the building, where the sidewalk was still in shadow. I crept across the street, wrapped my hands around the night-cold bars of the iron fence, and scanned the barren construction site. Big machines raised their fists to the sky, frozen in brutal choreography. The earth beneath them had been hacked and chewed and rearranged, revealing its essential lifelessness. Several varieties of cacti sat in black plastic pots, huddled on either side of a boulder that perhaps was not real. At its base lay a pale pink bundle—a tarp, or a heavy canvas cloth. I pressed my cheeks painfully into the bars. I stared at the bundle that now looked vaguely human. A breeze moved across it, and it appeared to take a breath.

Defeated, I began the long, hot walk back to the apartment. I wanted nothing more than to climb into bed and read the plain and powerful stories of my youth. I would fall asleep early, then rise again before the sun to meet myself as I really was.

By the time I got home, many sufferers had risen. Their blinds were raised, and they stood framed in their windows, pale-faced and blinking. Some were shuffling through the street toward their appointments. As usual, I took the stairs so as not to occupy the elevator, leaving it open for the ones who were not strong, and as I breathlessly ascended, it felt possible that I was approaching absolution.

I opened the door, which sucked a dry gust of wind from the open window, scattering the pages of the fax that was somehow still coming.

I approached the machine, my head aching in anticipation. A page emerged. It was totally black, almost radiant with darkness. The machine, it seemed, had malfunctioned. Marie had pushed it past its limit at last. Still, the longer I looked at the page, so dense with refusal, the more it seemed to contain an important message. I squinted, trying to read it. I rubbed my eyes. I held the page closer, then further away. I took it to the

window and angled it toward the light. I heard the sound of a
stranger calling up to me from the street, and a line of text rose
briefly to the surface, then disappeared.

*Although, I might just do the same thing again. The same
thing...*

Acknowledgments

Thank you to my friends and the children of my friends. To Adam Gardner, Angela Long, Amy Bonnaffons, Bettina Wohlfender, Caitie Moore, Caren Beilin, David Enos, Jennifer Panagos, Julie Bloom, Gabriel C. Drummond-Cole, Jackie Kari, Klon Waldrip, Lindsey Paulson, Maija Liisa Björklund, Nabil Kashyap, Neil Haydon, Pablo Lapegna, Shamala Gallagher, and Tag Savage. To dreams, Reginald McKnight, and Thérèse of Lisieux. To Ms. Mary and Silver River Elementary. To Bharati Mukherjee, Clarke Blaise, Debra Earling, Deirdre McNamer, and Ron Loewinsohn. To Kunstnarhuset Messen, California, and Tromsø. To Chris Kraus, Ellena Basada, Henning Howlid Wærp, Laura Preston, and Sabrina Orah Mark. To my mother, father, and brother. To the marsh, the cold ocean, and the garden. To Lola.

Stories in this collection have appeared in *BOMB*, *Boston Review*, *DIAGRAM*, *echoverse*, *Fence*, *The Georgia Review*, *Heavy Feather Review*, *Los Angeles Review of Books*, *McSweeney's*, *Prairie Schooner*, *A Public Space*, and *The White Review*.

FONO
GRAƎ

1. **Eileen Myles**—*Aloha/irish trees* (LP)

2. **Rae Armantrout**—*Conflation* (LP)

3. **Alice Notley**—*Live in Seattle* (LP)

4. **Harmony Holiday**—*The Black Saint and the Sinnerman* (LP)

5. **Susan Howe & Nathaniel Mackey**—*STRAY: A Graphic Tone* (LP)

6. **Annelyse Gelman & Jason Grier**—*About Repulsion* (EP)

7. **Joshua Beckman**—*Some Mechanical Poems To Be Read Aloud* (print)

8. **Dao Strom**—*Instrument/ Traveler's Ode* (print; cassette tape)

9. **Douglas Kearney & Val Jeanty**—*Fodder* (LP)

10. **Mark Leidner**—*Returning the Sword to the Stone* (print)

11. **Charles Valle**—*Proof of Stake: An Elegy* (print)

12. **Emily Kendal Frey**—*LOVABILITY* (print)

13. **Brian Laidlaw and the Family Trade**—*THIS ASTER: adaptations of Emile Nelligan* (LP)

14. **Nathaniel Mackey and The Creaking Breeze Ensemble**—*Fugitive Equation* (compact disc)

15. *FE Magazine* (print)

16. **Brandi Katherine Herrera**—*MOTHER IS A BODY* (print)

17. **Jan Verberkmoes**—*Firewatch* (print)

18. **Krystal Languell**—*Systems Thinking with Flowers* (print)

19. **Matvei Yankelevich**—*Dead Winter* (print)

20. **Cody-Rose Clevidence**—*Dearth & God's Green Mirth* (print)

21. **Hilary Plum**—*Hole Studies* (print)

22. **John Ashbery**—*Live at Sanders Theatre, 1976* (LP)

23. **Alice Notley**—*The Speak Angel Series* (print)

24. **Alice Notley**—*Early Works* (print)

25. **Joshua Marie Wilkinson**—*Trouble Finds You* (print)

26. **Timmy Straw**—*The Thomas Salto* (print)

27. **Audre Lorde**—*At Fassett Studio, 1970* (LP)

28. **Gabriel Palacios**—*A Ten Peso Burial For Which Truth I Sign* (print)

29. **Isabel Zapata, trans. Robin Myers**—*A Whale Is a Country* (print)

30. **Callum Angus**—*Cataract* (print)

31. **Eds. Dao Strom & Jyothi Natarajan**—*A Mouth Holds Many Things: A De-Canon Hybrid-Literary Collection* (print)

32. **Cody-Rose Clevidence**—*The Grimace of Eden, Now* (print)

33. **Jaydra Johnson**—*Low: Notes on Art and Trash* (print)

34. **Jaime Gil de Biedma**—*If Only For a Moment (I'll Never Be Young Again)* (print)

35. **Esther Kondo Heller**—*AR:RANGE:MENTS* (print)

36. **Ahmad Almallah**—*Wrong Winds* (print)

37. **Kimberly Alidio**—*Traceable Relation* (print)

38. **Sara Gilmore**—*The Green Lives* (print)

39. **Darcie Dennigan**—*Little Neck* (print)

40. **Nora Claire Miller**—*Groceries* (print)

41. **Rachel Rahmé**—*Mercurial, or is that Liberty?* (print)

42. **Eileen Myles**—*Bird Watching and Their First Three Books of Poetry* (print)

Fonograf Editions is a registered 501(c)(3) nonprofit organization. Find more information about the press at: fonografeditions.com.